The Episodes:

www.inejiro.tokyo

The Second Edition

Cover Design by Patrick F Waters
Edited by Val Bilotti

www.inejiro.tokyo
www.luxarium.info

ISBN-13: 978-1-957174-05-1
Kalyanji-Mandeep
Published by Coffin & Crown LTD

Original Music at
soundcloud.com/deeproy

<u>Amplify:</u> [**am**-pl*uh*-fahy] (v) 1. To make larger, greater, or stronger.

In 2115 The UN takes notice of the inability of its member states to properly govern their people. Riots, protests, and political assassinations have led up to a catastrophic event in the 53rd state, the San Francisco Bay Area, which forced the UN to step in.

Now the war is over and countries loyal to their UN membership have recovered and are on the rise. This anthology tours the globe, giving readers insight into the bizarre goings-on now that 70% of the planet lives under one government.

Plant hybrids, masked gangsters, time travel, super science. All episodes in this series connect and shed light on each other.

For You

"The Customer is always right..."

...EPISODE 8

ACT I

SEASON 27

WEEK 1

THE TEAMS

Divisions

THE HAVES	THE HAVE NOTS
Prime	Hoi Polloi
LA	Munich
Rome	Saigon
Estes Park	Bangkok
The UN	Tashkent
Nova	Plebian
DC	Mumbai
Tokyo	Miami
Incan Empire	Chicagoland
London	Mexico City
Alpha	Prole
San Fu-Kuo	Assam
Cairo	NY
Sydney	Ottawa
Paris	Moscow

TEAM NAMES

Prime	Hoi Polloi
Los Angeles, CE Law Firm	Meunchen Teutonishen Maschine
The Roman Legion	Saigon Amalgamated Clanship
Estes Park Simulacra	Bangkok Royal Mass Hysteria
The UN Global Alliance	Tashkent Sharmacorp Miasamtic Plague
Nova	**Plebian**
Dioecesis Columbium Old Glory	Mumbai Federation Of Scientists
Edo (Tokyo) TASC Masters	Miami United Workers Party
Restored Incan Empire Obsidian Pumas	Chicagoland Organized Labor
London Amplified Gentry	Mexico City V^2 Immortals
Alpha	**Prole**
San Fu-Kuo Mitsune-gumi Ronin	Assam Creeping Death
Cairo Twice-Risen Pharaohs	NY Illuminati
Sydney Copper Locusts	Ottawa Iron Maples
Paris Reign of Terror	Moscow Atomic Energy Federation

THE RULES:

Scoring:

Touchdowns:
- 6 Points Standard
- 8 Points within final 10 seconds of 1st half
- 10 Points within final 10 seconds of game
- Must break the plane.
- Extra Points from 30-meter line
- 2-Point Conversions allowed from 5-meter line

Field Goals:
- 3 Points Standard
- 5 Points final 10 seconds of game
- Missed Field Goals result in a free rouge point for the other team
- Kickable at any time*, by any one$^{\Delta}$

*NO GAME MAY BE DECIDED BY A FIELD GOAL.
$^{\Delta}$if try is missed, loss of possession occurs.

THE RULES:

Gameplay:

- If a specific rule is not mentioned, default to current Canadian rule.
- 4-Down System
- 12 on 12
- Men, Women, Robots, Simulacra, are ALL eligible to play
- Forward passes are allowed from anywhere behind Standard AND Auxiliary Lines of Scrimmage
- No Holding, False Starts, or Illegal Formations
- Pass Interference occurs after 10 meters
- Push-Offs are allowed
- All Linemen are ALWAYS eligible
- No "Lineman Downfield" penalty
- Missed/Blocked FGs, Punts, Extra Points are all returnable
- "One Foot" for ALL catches
- ALL penalty calls are reviewable
- ALL plays are reviewable
- "Force Out" rule is active
- Not "playing the ball" WILL NOT result in Pass Interference
- WR are allowed running starts before snap
- A catch occurs regardless of a "football move"
- A catch occurs regardless of loss of control by player while going to the ground.

11

THE RULES:

Players:

- Numbers are arbitrary, with certain exceptions
- 3-digit jersey numbers and "00" are allowed
- ALL players are cross-trained for Offence and Defense according to their strengths
- ALL players play opposing positions during Spring League
- No personal doctors, trainers, or spiritual advisers are allowed on-field or in team facilities at any time
- Lavish TD celebrations are allowed and encouraged
- HGH and other Performance Enhancing Drugs are ALL allowed, standardized, regulated, and supervised
- Players can be put up as prizes to increase the stakes of winning.

1QB: Prime Quarterback
2QB: Nova Quarterback
1WR: Prime Wide-Receiver
1FB: Prime Fullback
1RB: Prime Running Back
1SS: Prime Strong Safety
1FS: Prime Free Safety
1CB: Prime Cornerback

1LT: Prime Left Tackle
1LG: Prime Left Guard
1C: Prime Center
1RG: Prime Right Guard
1RT: Prime Right Tackle
OLB: Outside Linebacker
1DE: Prime Defensive End
1NT: Prime Nose Tackle

THE RULES:

Power Ups:

- Power Ups, or "chits", come with wins and or achievements
- Chits can be 'staked' and bound to game results; i.e. chits may be bet/given as prizes for beating certain teams
- Wheel of Enrichment: Spun but a lottery chosen fan at the start of each match, this probability engine generates a circumstance that must be affect the entire game.

A Selection of Chits:

- STUCK: 1 sticky glove for 1 player for 1 quarter
- JAIL: remove 1 player for 1 quarter
- GROUNDED: No passing plays for 1 Half
- FLIGHT: No running plays for 1 Half
- MULTIBALL: 3 extra balls added for 1 play. All balls are eligible for scoring.
- NEXT MAN UP: Upside down depth chart for 1 quarter
- SOD: Re-sod the field at Half Time
- GROWTH: A mature redwood tree will be planted anywhere on the field, at coach's discretion.

THE RULES:

Base Deployment:

Offence
2 QBs
2 WRs
1 RB
1 FB
5 Linemen
1 TE

Defense
2 NTs
2 Ends
4 LBs
2 Safeties
2 CBs

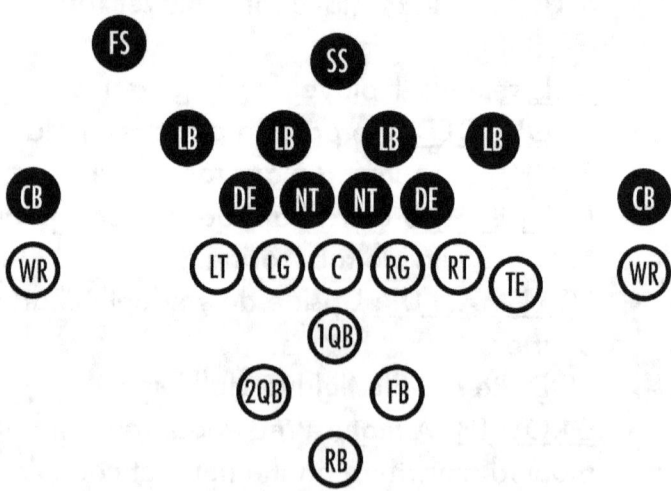

THE RULES:

The Field:

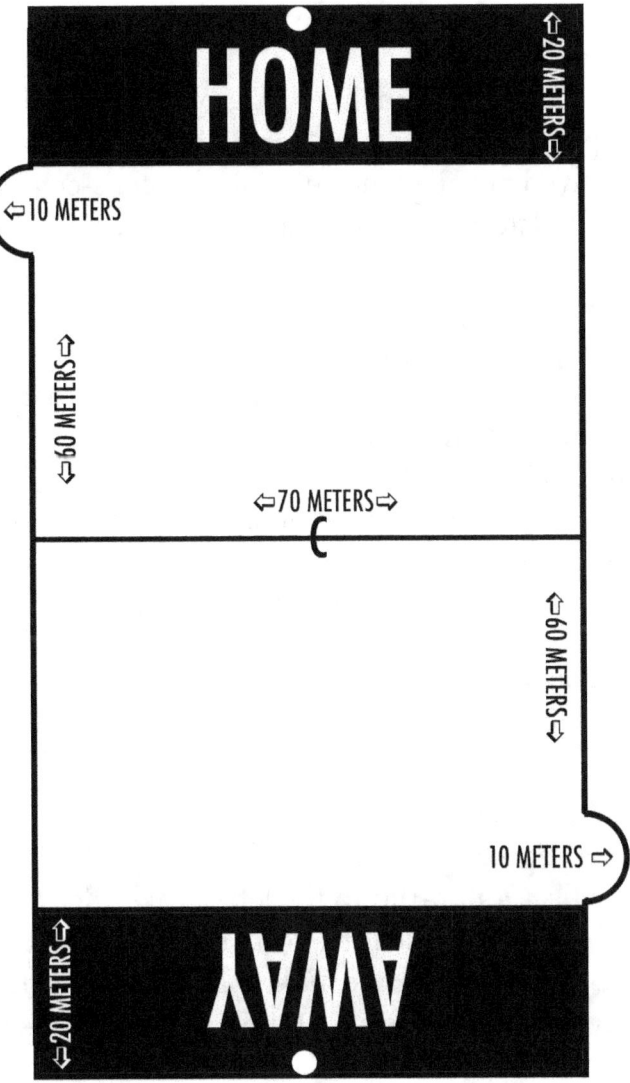

THE TRANSFERENCE OF
CHARLEMAGNE ARCENEAUX-WANG

It was Third down.

1QB The Amplified Napoleon Bonaparte took his spot in the shotgun behind his Maginot-Minded offensive line. His blue and gold officer's-coat-themed jersey bolstered the cerulean in his eyes. The tails of the coat portion flapped in the gentle breeze. The embroidered gold *999* below his nameplate glistened in the light of the sun. In the span of five ticks on the play clock he solved the defensive puzzle that formed on the frontier beyond. He sharply bellowed individualized audibles.

1WR Remy Ouattara ambled his wiry frame to a slot position.

1FB Chevalier Le Pen moved from beside Bonaparte and settled on the weak side next to 1TE Pierre Cong Diep.

1RB Charlemagne Arceneaux-Wang quietly replaced Le Pen.

The snap.

Napoleon caught the ball with one hand and began his Option-run to the left, weak, side.

As he rounded the corner, Le Pen collided with collapsing 1FS Antonio Fujimoto. The animated Free Safety diagnosed the Option Play as Bonaparte directed his pre-snap players. The gap these two crumbling behemoths created was enough for

Bonaparte to squirt into a pocket of open field, Arceneaux-Wang in close pursuit.

After three frantic meters, Bonaparte makes the pitch to Arceneaux-Wang. He in turn makes the catch in-stride and quickly jukes past Nickel-CB Dontarii Glover.

The magenta glowing First Down line is in reach. There are only two players to beat.

After pealing off an unseen hold from star wide-out Ouattara, speedy MLB Wilbur Thompson set his sights on the blue blur in coat tails proudly bearing the number seven.

It was too late.

Number seven crossed the First Down line.

In front of him was the final obstacle.

The crowd was erupting with joy at the player's wild downfield ambulation.

1SS Conrad Atwater was at the threshold of putting the effectiveness of his positional title to the test.

Charlemagne faked left, planted on his right, and spun directly into Atwater. Undaunted, he continued his march towards the end zone, now a mere twelve meters away. His thick legs churned against Atwater and reminded him of trying to operate an old combustion automobile with the parking brake still fully engaged.

The first closest defender was Thompson. Still angry about the missed penalty, he chose to simply lower his shoulders and blow up both players. However, after yelling a battle cry and announcing his presence, Charlemagne Arceneaux-Wang twisted and placed Atwater into prime position to absorb the hit. Thompson shattered Atwater's grip and the two defenders became but as chaff.

Alas, the degree to which Charlemagne had been slowed had allowed the heaving mass of defense at his back to catch up.

He was wrapped and twisted by the team leader in interceptions, 1CB Fumiko Tamura. She sharply whipped her head around, Charlemagne in tow. Her radiant black hair at last followed in an overtly elegant display of an all-consuming and cold deluge.

As he was brought into a closer, albeit unwanted, relationship with the humming earth, a specific and resonating misfortune occurred. Tamura's zealous tackle, textbook as it may have been, had placed Charlemagne in the path of a defender who overshot his approach and, during his attempt to avoid collision, managed to strike Charlemagne in the head.

Lavender.

Cold, hard floor.

Plain white rafters reflecting soft, equally white, light.

"He's back!"

Two ruddy-looking men in long sleeved orange thick cotton shirts pulled Charlemagne to his feet.

He forced himself to detach his fixation from their perfect curled handlebar mustaches and surveyed the other players.

Where are their pads?

All around him were what must have been his teammates. He surmised this after noticing the very same heavy orange cotton on his own skin. An equally orange number seven was sewn onto a black shield-shaped piece of similar material that was itself buttoned onto the main garment. He ran his hand down the front and noted that the black bib-like attachment was large went down to his navel.

"You sure he's *all the way* back?" An unfamiliar voice chided nearby.

He felt the ball still in his hands and looked at it. This was not The Nabob, the official PolyMatic Ball. Instead he saw the word 'DUKE' just below the laces.

His hands were his.

This fact was established by confirming the existence of a scar given him by a steam press in his grandfather's custom laundry service.

"C'mon, pal, game's still on!" A referee in green and white stripes and a sparkling gold cap urged Charlemagne to give him the ball. After several brief nanoseconds of assessment, he gave over the leathery construct like a reflex and trotted over to what was apparently his huddle.

The Quarterback knelt down in the center and called the play radioed in from the coach standing in the back of the end zone.

"Chanticleer 9, viper cliff with a *moonshot*, break!"

Charlemagne had no idea what play had been called.

The linemen trotted out and assumed a Traditional deployment. The tight end lined up on the strong side. Two receivers lined up on the weak side, while a third lined up far away on the strong. Charlemagne counted his teammates; there were eleven.

Only eleven players per-side? He thought.

He counted the defense and arrived at the same number.

The snap.

The quarterback expertly walked Charlemagne through play-action and side-armed a pass to the back shoulder of the bulky tight end. He spun around in perfect sync and caught it before being powerfully sandwiched between two defenders.

Charlemagne marveled as all players involved sprang right up from the floor, despite it being hardwood. He then realized he was wearing *regular shoes*. He looked down and saw rubberized spikes that began on the top of the toes and curled under the front, leading all the way to the heel. All the players had similar footwear. They all also wore Knickerbocker socks, leather helmets (if they wore helmets at all), elaborate facial hair, breeches, and no padding of any kind.

And yet these men, and *only* men, were bounding off of the visibly unyielding surface of the hardwood floor.

That's when he felt his own boisterous growth of facial hair. It hung on his face like an accessory and he could feel a lithe separation between the villus construct and his skin.

A quadrilateral, mechanical-looking scoreboard with buzzing variables made legible by Nixie vacuum tubes indicated to the tightly-packed and balconied crowd it was 3rd down and four yards to go.

Another huddle.

"*Dispassionate Imp* with a yellow thumb screw, on three, break!"

The other players chuckled at the call.

Charlemagne lined up on the wrong side.

"This side, wise guy," the impressively tall QB instructed.

The instant Charlemagne corrected, the snap occurred.

The ball was fed to his stomach.

His feet started driving forward by rote.

A hole appeared between a tackle and guard, he stepped in, but a hefty defender appeared.

He spun out and found his Full Back, who vociferously blazed a trail through the cacophony that had developed in the flat.

Another reflex, his sturdy stiff arm, thwarted an imposing vermillion-clad defender.

He was home free.

The end zone he trotted into was bolstered by the opposing team and its coaching staff. He spun around from the snarling faces set against him and noticed the opposite end zone was surrounded and backed by men, and *only* men, wearing uniforms like his. These two groups of men separated by the field of play were the only 'field level' spectators, and the only ones making *any* noise.

He turned away from the sneering cadre and looked up at the spectators. There were two narrow dark wooden balconies on either side of the building they were all in. They contained very well dressed men *and* women. The people were stone-faced and silent. Half wore orange finery, the others the intense red of the visiting team.

He trotted back to the opposite end of the field and was welcomed to his end zone with cheers from his teammates.

"READY!" The barrel-chested Center called.

"S! T! E! A! M! RRRRRRROOOOOLLLLLLLEEERRRRR!"

The entire orange and black collective roared as one.

A dingy white humanoid, dog-ish, mascot in a very tired looking orange cardigan stood sexless at the vanguard. It fearlessly leered at the other mascot, a heaving red bird wearing a halo and a habit. This display served as the customary post-score celebration. Across the white man-dog's back was an intricate orange and black tapestry depicting a gargantuan steamroller on a rampage with the word PROVIDENCE carved into the roll.

The buzzing tube scoreboard informed anyone who happened to be looking at it that the Providence

Steamroller was up seventeen points over the ChicagOrleans St. Cardinals.

The team names were ancient, as was the style of play.

Charlemagne drank from the cup that was handed him; some sort of basic electrolyte solution with a lemony flavor. There were no healing pods. No narcoplants. No quick-cryo chambers. No digireal field.

But it was football.

Just not the PolyMatic brand he had dedicated his life to.

"False Start, number seventy eight, ten yards, still first down," the green and gold referees announcement interrupted his stream of thoughts.

A False Start? Charlemagne was baffled. That penalty, along with a host of others, had been eliminated from his realm many years prior.

The St. Cardinals QB took a seven-step drop back from under center, also unusual for Charlemagne's eyes, and whipped a bullet pass while leaping.

A Sainted Cardinal wearing a white leather helmet with a red crest shoved a Providence defender down as he extended his body and made the catch, crashing into the wood paneled wall that served as a sideline at full speed. He got right up and caught the flashing brown penalty flag that was thrown at him with disdain.

"Pass Interference, Offense number eleven, Unsportsmanlike Conduct, throwing the officials flag, also Offense number eleven, the two 15-yard penalties will combine, repeat first down."

Whoa...

The game continued on with Charlemagne figuring out the plays as needed.

The final score was The Providence Steamroller 52, The ChicagOrleans St. Cardinals 30.

In the locker room Charlemagne watched the other men disengage their mustaches. When they did, a shimmering green outline appeared and then dissipated from around their body like an evaporating blanket.

He touched his face and gave the protrusion a tug. It resisted like a magnet for a brief second then came off with a muted click. The green particles became fireflies and vanished.

He turned to ask the man next to him about the device, but was met by a staunch finger to the mouth, indicating the need to be silent.

He was almost done changing when he felt the subtlest tap on his shoulder.

A man dressed in a Steamroller orange bellhop uniform.

The man smiled and handed Charlemagne a check.

It was made out to him, despite never having seen these people before this day.

GD$700,000

"For one game?!" He shouted in joyful disbelief. The amount was staggering.

"Shhh!" Came a locker room chorus of

24

quietude.

He finished up and followed the other men to what he assumed was the exit. Before he was through the doors, he was handed a thin hard piece of metal.

HANDEGG SCHEDULE 3139

FOR YOUR EYES ONLY!

All Games Kickoff At 1400hrs *sharp!*

Oct 4
v. Old New York

Oct 11
v. Ft. Dallas

Oct 18
v. ChicagOrleans

Oct 25
v. CinciCleveland...

There were sixteen games in total.
All on Tuesdays.
All at two in the afternoon.
Before it could all sink in, he found himself

being shuffled out of the facility along with several others.

He next found himself out on the street. The men who emerged from the faceless warehouse alongside him all went separate directions. No one made eye contact. No one spoke.

Charlemagne wrote the number, 56, that hung above the non-descript door that led into the non-descript white building in this drab and desolate part of wherever he may be.

It was six o'clock in the evening. The digital clock hanging in a dirty window told him so.

He picked a direction and began walking.

He eventually came upon a more active part of the city and decided it was time to convert his promissory note into transactable currency.

The bank that matched the logo on the check readily accepted his DNA identification and issued him a debit wristband.

With such a swollen new bank account, he had no trouble walking in off the street and renting an apartment. The eagerness of the building management firm seemed odd, but so did literally everything else he had experienced up to this point. He memorized the route to the facility and began thinking of ways to reach out to the people whom he knew.

Just as he dialed one of the few phone numbers he had memorized, a knock came at the door.

He got up and asked through the door, "Who is it?"

"Please, Mr. Wang, open the door," a woman's

voice.

There was no peephole, but there was a chain. He cracked the door open and slipped an eye out.

She was overwhelmingly beautiful. She smirked and he mechanically opened the door, mesmerized by her energy.

Her presence filled the entire apartment space.

"Mr. Wang, I represent the Agency that has brought you here. While I'm not at liberty to disclose where 'here' is, I can assure you that your loved ones are fine. But, I must also bear bad news as you are barred from seeing them again.

"Excuse me?"

"You're excused, but I'm not done talking. Mr. Wang, you were *chosen* because of your phenomenal performance for The Reign Of Terror over the past several years. Our handlers have decided you need to be a part of *our* organization from here on out. We will provide you with a proper living space, food, women, clothing, everything you need. All you need to do, sir, is play, and play *hard*."

Charlemagne began dialing the same number.

"It's no use, Mr. Wang. Please don't hurt yourself."

Playing under a cloned Napoleon Bonaparte had afforded Charlemagne the ability to adjust to receiving command-level orders with no explanation. He exhaled through his nose and simply nodded. He turned away from the severe woman and looked out the window. The city was large. Both the landscape and architecture were very unusual. Everything had a crisp newness to it.

"May I at least know where I am?"

"Sure, to an extent. *You*, for all intents and purposes are in the city of Providence, capital of this Section of New Sparta."

"*New Sparta?*" Charlemagne was incredulous.

"Hmm, yes. Now get on the bed. Take off your clothes…"

Charlemagne swallowed hard as the woman advanced on him, and the door to his apartment shut on its own.

1

THE FAN

IT was a Tuesday.

The canned music oozed from the speakers woven into the freestanding shelving units that ultimately comprised the aisles. Overhead, several green and silver pendant lights hung down, their retro-dusted incandescent light bathing all below.

"No, no they don't go like that. They *can't* go like that," the man's weathered arms and sturdy hands moved like expertly guided machinery.

The Level II Clerk took a step back to allow the intruding King to reorganize the row of truffle oil bottles. The pale, small, man brushed a few invisible specks from his neatly creased vest and ran his tongue across the front of his teeth. He next turned his gaze to the gray and white linoleum floor for a second and a half. Around them, other shoppers pushed their yellow acrylic shopping carts past and carried on.

"Bianci, then Nero, then the French bottles…" Each bottle was carefully repositioned into perfect, solider-like alignment.

The Clerk marveled at the lines in the King's hands in the light that flowed from the low-hanging lamp overhead. His shirt was pressed and the stitching on his logo, just above the left breast, was impeccable. His shoes bore no laces. His pants never once wrinkled in the slightest. Even his diadem, modeled after an Egyptian deshret, looked so crisp and clean it was like a hologram. It was strikingly evident this man had put in the required hours and devotion to reach his station. Even the way he had injected himself into the Clerk's duties was cordial, considerate. The dedication and poise his position commanded… *Clearly this man should be revered!*

"There. Perfect," the bald pink-skinned Texan reviewed his handiwork through the thin slits that served for eyes. His tongue made a brief appearance to moisten his toothpick of an upper lip.

"What's yer name, son?" The King asked without looking, his voice a velvet and gravel river.

"Nikolaus Ito Sanzenbacher, sir."

"Kee-ripes son that's a mouthful. They didn't shorten it when you were first brought in?"

"Yes sir they did, Niko-San."

"Excellent. How long have you been *Ensconced?*"

"This is my sixth moon."

"Six moons, eh? And you're already a mark II?" The King was noticeably intrigued by this. From the moment he turned down this aisle during his Inspection he was fixated on this comparatively young man bearing the distinctive gold stripes of a Level II.

"Yes sir. I excelled at stocking and crafting attractive end cap displays."

"Did you? Well, because you took my counsel without attitude, today's your lucky day..."

Niko hesitated to believe the high-ranking man.

"Today Niko-san, you're moving to the register," the King said. Placing his heavy and dry right hand on the small-statured Clerk's shoulder, he withdrew a pod from a pocket on the front of his shimmering green apron. The King next depressed a soft red button, causing the pod to split and spring open. From within, a golden dragonfly spread its wings and hovered over to Niko.

The ruby eyes flittered and clicked as the insect took in Niko's face, matching it to the one in the database. Once confirmed, the dragonfly would send the upgrade signal, raising the Clerk to Level III, the ultimate of this particular sphere. Niko admired the intricate filigree along the segmented abdomen. The gradual parts of this mechanized creature made him think of the ladder he was climbing.

Working the register was the springboard to General Manager. Once you were a GM, you no longer needed to Stock the Store, which really meant more prestige and recognition for your station.

Niko had put in a bit more time than he had initially led on, but he really only felt like the last six months counted. His heart just wasn't in it before then.

He had initially come in purely out of curiosity. He had no 'in.' Niko was old school. He enjoyed the moribund, nearly bygone method of social engineering: trawling the Ultra Net for the hidden truths about the world that now surrounded him. He had honed his skills after a particularly embarrassing 'exposé' of his local dentist. He recovered from the witch-hunt and learned to ignore his gut and to use his discerning wit as a filter for truth amongst the sea of lies that were message boards.

"...SO you think you got it?"

"Yeah, I can do this. Thank you for the opportunity, your majesty."

"Hehe, boy I tell ya… They just don't make 'em like you any more. The Customer's always right."

"The Customer's always right," Niko said with a smile.

The King and his entourage turned and walked away in the direction of this store's Grand Kitchen.

For a time Niko wondered if King Clancy remembered bringing him in, or if his asking about his time Shopping was a clever ruse to detect plants and moles. Either way, Niko was rising through the ranks and this stopover at the register ringing up the other Customers would serve him well for the time being.

After his shift, Niko decided to skip the walk and take a rickshaw. Yes it cost a bit of coin, but the rigors of training at a new position at his Store had put a damper on his desire to walk. The driver was from Nepal. Niko put in his earbuds and played the latest Handgun For An Ape album. The driving double-bass drums and the 9/8 timed sitar and tabla were aural perfection

He arrived and glided through the small, brown, and ratty lobby to the dingy communal spiral stairs that led to his door. Back home in his shared apartment, Niko took to researching his favorite pastime when a bit of supplemental information caught his eye.

He had been deeply examining the persistence of zombie lore in a modern, reasoning, society.

"Zombies? *In Mexico?*" Niko had found an old, much-disputed post that purported to detail a rather grisly experience about a farm hand named Rolando.*

Niko couldn't believe it.

He read, and re-read the story several times, committing it to memory. He wasn't sure what it was that made it so special. Something in the prose, something in the order of events; it was like he could close his eyes and see it. He took a screenshot and started asking other trusted anon's what they knew. After a few days of fascination, he remembered his secure inbox.

He reasoned that he could use this mailbox to perhaps digitally pantomime an interest in the investment potential of the region. *Assam has a world-class football team, so why not elite professional wrestling?* Was his rhetorical bait. He ultimately hoped his casting a line into the digital sea would merely return some tractionable information.

Then he remembered the last time he actually used that address.

*http://bit.ly/ROLMEX

It was three years prior.

"Ssso, ssso, yy-you can do it?"

"Yeah, man. I said I could. Here's the address,"

Niko handed the spastic man from Shenzhen a scrap of paper:

00216754398478@oOoI/.xt

"That paper dissolves in water so *be careful.* No sweating."

The man grunted and nodded in rapid succession. "Ddd-don't forget the *package*! Iiiii-it has arrived…"

Niko eyed the filthy man.

This job had been particularly unusual. Niko was to put on a green butcher's coat and false mustache, walk down an alley whistling an old addictive commercial jingle, and simply collect a plastic shopping bag full of groceries. The bag was then to be dropped off at a hotel that was putting up the world champion Ethiopian Cricket Team.

He returned home and opened the package that had been delivered during his meeting with the fidgety Chinese. He set the duct-tape-entombed box on the coffee table and sliced it open. In the box there was dirty clothing and a facial hair prosthesis. After getting dressed, he noticed how much like his client he looked. The grimy little man in burlap and leather never told him he would be a stand-in, but then again Niko didn't put it together in his mind while talking to him, and he wasn't quite sure why. From the very beginning he felt compelled to take this job. He *needed* to work for this sketchy man from Shenzhen.

As he stood in the mirror, trying to understand how he could overlook such an obvious connection, his computer dinged.

An orange '1' lit up his secure inbox.

The message had the two agreed upon words:

Go time.

The air was crisp but tight. He took the Worker's bus to a northern and strange part of London. Taking a Civic bus would've drawn too much unwanted attention to the way he was dressed.

Niko didn't recognize the name of the district surrounding the address he had been given. The lights were not the bright white of his locale; they were orange and grating. The shop windows were too dark to notice any real detail. There were actual telephone poles and wiring crisscrossing the entire zone. Several brief stops along the way allowed him to make out a few store fronts. There was an odd arrangement of dolls beneath a single red incandescent light bulb in one window. Another window box, lit with red and green incandescent light bulbs, displayed an illegal shrine of some sort.

After twenty minutes of creaking turns down

narrow streets that forced him to lean on other grimy men and women, the driver abruptly stopped the bus in the middle of an intersection.

At first, the other passengers assumed a hazard in the road of some sort. After ten minutes, however, the sea became restless.

"Oi, Wot's tha bleedin' problem, mate?"

No answer.

"Dis guy… BLOKE! I AM SPEAKING AT YOU! MOVE THIS BUS!"

"No. Way." The thick Cape Town accent shut down any hopes for a speedy continuation.

Niko checked his watch. There was still plenty of time. But the unfamiliarity of this part of London and the angry people encasing him onboard made him anxious.

C'mon… Just go!

"I am not moving an *inch!*"

"I just did twelve hours on a C.R.E.W. lunch galley, YOU ARE MOVIN' THIS BUS!" A large black woman was pushing her way towards the driver's cage.

For a brief second, Niko thought of abandoning this bus and finishing his delivery on foot. He craned is neck around and took a look through the graffitied window only to focus on the nearest street corner. A cackling dwarf was perched atop a set of strange looking stilts. He wore a dingy lime green kimono with red piping. The dwarf rubbed his hands and concealed a bloody knife in his sleeve. Not too far off, Niko could see a hand and forearm, missing the rest of the body, just laying, out in the open, on the street. Niko elected to stay put until the driver continued.

The arguing intensified.

More tired working-class people were rallying behind the large, angry, black woman every second.

She approached the cage.

"Sir, I am tired. We are all tired. We've done our jobs. Now, you need to do *your* job."

"The union cut my hours! They cut my hours, I cut their *throat!*" The South African raised a hand in exclamation. The woman shot her arm though the cage bars and seized his appendage. The blood from her nails, dugs deep into his flesh, began to pool at their feet.

"I-"

"Sir," she said in a calm and steady voice. "You need to start driving…"

"Oi, mate, depress the gas pedal already…"

The standoff lasted another thirty seconds.

The driver, his arm still ensnared, engaged the controls, and resumed driving his route. Applause rose from the passengers. Niko did his best to shake off the laughing dwarf, having accidently made eye contact with him. The dwarf whooped and smiled at Niko until they were out of each others field of vision.

He got off the bus and followed the path that was laid out for him by the Chinese. He turned down several alleys that had odd-smelling noodle stands strewn amongst old VHS dens and the occasional black market liquor and tobacconist. At one stand a group of women were gorging themselves on bowls of ramen topped with a thick layer of duck fat. As they grazed, several LED screens blared various things from news to sumo to Word League of Intoxicated Automobiling highlights.

Niko passed through the throng and arrived at the address the man had scrawled out for him.

He did as he had prepared and knocked a syncopated eight times on the wooden door.

Nothing happened.

Niko waited, and waited.

After a time, he realized he had never seen this part of London before. Everything was so… *Japanese*. In fact, the house he stood in front of had rice paper and bamboo walls, as did all the other row houses in this area.

The roads were too narrow for cars.

A memory flickered on.

He was in Tokyo, Setagaya to be exact, with his mother. She was dragging him along down alley after alley. They seemed to turn every five or six steps.

He never forgot the architecture.

Suddenly, back in London, the door slid open.

A man, in a blue and gold Mexican wrestling mask, greeted him with eyes like open manholes.

Wordlessly the man extended a plastic shopping bag. A logo Niko couldn't quite make out was on it. He could, however, see the slogan.

The Customer is ALWAYS right. ALWAYS.

He took the bag and the door slid shut. Just as before he arrived, there was no sound coming from the thin-walled building.

Niko turned and felt a sense of panic wash over him. *Why is the bag so heavy?*

His next destination, thankfully, did not require a bus ride. He grafted himself into the leviathan of people during the 0100am shift change.

No one looked at each other.

No one noticed Niko, or his bag.

He kept his eyes peeled, out of habit, but no one was coming after him.

He saw a sign indicating his need to leave the heaving mass, and did so.

Something bumped the bag, and he heard a grunt.

Just as he developed the thought of *looking* into the bag, he noticed he had arrived at his destination.

A single door, in the middle of the broad side of a large brick warehouse greeted him. Niko looked around and quickly saw that he was in a very remote and lonely area. The awkwardly narrow roads and lack of human life remained the standard, as did the web of electrical wires that poured out of every construct. The orange light from the street lamps clung to the unfamiliar buildings.

He looked at the door.

It was exactly like the doors he had passed through an innumerable amount of times while shopping for candy, or clothes, or groceries. He had never seen *this* door before, but its innate familiarity was more palpable than the empty breeze blowing only on him.

It was green glass with a metal frame.

In front, a convenient and readily accessible push bar curved in decline from just above a keyhole on the right, over to the left-most hinge. Behind the glass were curtains, and behind that, darkness.

A single sign hung, at an angle, in the middle of the upper portion:

"What?" Niko said out loud.

He checked his own piece of water-soluble paper for the address and despite the runny ink, this was the spot.

He looked around once more, then back at the sign.

The bag he held shuddered.

That didn't just happen… he told himself.

One more time, he scoured the kitschy door for anything he might have missed.

An asterisk next to the exclamation point.

He found its correspondent near the bottom left of the sign, in bafflingly small print:

*In a rush? Ring the bell!

He spotted a small white button with a dingy gold frame.

One more look around at the desolation.

The buttons soft rubber betrayed the rigid surroundings.

The moment his finger left the posh tree-distillate, the door flung open.

Another man in a luchador mask.

The two stood, blankly staring into each other's souls.

The luchador hiccupped. His pristine orange snakeskin suit was slowly getting stained by an emerging thick, translucent, green goo.

"Uh, de-Delivery, sir," Niko cleared his throat and deepened his voice.

Nothing.

"H-hello? I have this bag and I-"

The man's hand rose in acceptance.

Niko reflexively handed him the plastic sack, getting a nanosecond's glance at the innards. A single eye's gaze met his.

It blinked.

The luchador continued looking past Niko and returned his arm to his side of the portal. The door closed, and Niko was alone again, set upon by the silence and emptiness of this strange and obtuse part of London.

It took forty-five minutes for him to reach an area with enough wireless reception to get a call out for a black cab.

The fee was astronomical, as the ride home was well over four hours.

Three years ago.

He was still desperate for work beyond his full-time schedule at LeRoy's Narcofloria, just no longer *that* desperate.

Niko had told others about his experience in the mysterious, never-to-be-seen-again, portion of London. The severed, possibly living, head in the bag; the luchador and his chartreuse emissions were always saved for the end. No one believed him. All posts he shared were written off. It seemed like the more he tried to understand that courier job in London, the more fantastic the entire experience became.

Niko tabled his cybernetic fishing trip idea and instead chose to take his zombified findings to his coworkers at LeRoy's.

Niko hopped up from his computer and grabbed his device. The air outside was warm and the lobby of his building was full of the same faceless every day Assamese. His rickshaw home from his Store was a treat, so the walk from his building to his emporium was brisk and relaxing. The emporium was open, as it always was, and Niko trotted in just after a flock of college girls.

He looked around for Dev, Git, Sanjay, Sato, Prakhash, Neela, Dave, Paolo… None of the other regular employees were immediately present.

Instead, he found a new girl.

"Hello, my name is Niko."

"Hi, I'm Mariflor! I just moved here from Mexico City…" she continued on, but Niko was stuck on her city of origin.

"I'm sorry," he cut her off. "You said you were from Mexico City?" The fire of Rolando's Tale went from smoking kindling to a roaring blaze.

"Yes… I did," she was weary because of his sudden burst.

"This may be a little forward, but have you ever heard of Xavier El Burro?"

The name shook Mariflor.

"Who do you think you are? What are you trying to get from me?" Mariflor was justifiably on the defensive. Several nearby customers looked over to see what the commotion was.

"What? N-nothing, I just, I'm a huge fan of Lucha Libre, like, otaku level, and… and…" he decided to go for it. "I was wondering if you knew of any truth to the rumors about zombies in-"

"Zombies!? Are you serious?"

Mariflor scrunched up her face in revulsion and ran to the Employee's Only section of the emporium.

His reputation was destroyed after that.

Mariflor made sure everyone in the facility

knew where Niko's head was at any given moment.

After a week of whispers and disapproving stares, Niko had had enough antagonization. He decided to see for himself, in person, if the rumors and various posts that he had been recklessly citing had any substance.

He booked a flight and left.

He was unable to afford a quick and easy Rosenbridge Transfer. The time he got to himself on the plane, though, was a much needed respite from the constant buzzing that was modern day Assam. The airport looked like a used shoe outlet. The walls were stained wood paneling. There was that short-pile carpet that you would see in a dentist's office. The flight was due to take around twenty hours. Niko sighed when he calculated the math and bought a few issues of the latest Lucha Libre rags. There was SLAM!, Leg Lock Monthly, MasksMasksMasks, and the official magazine of Los Volcanes, La V^2 Voz. The glossy pictures and widely opinionated articles would provide a steady flow of entertainment. On the other side of the gate there was a LeRoy's Nano Tent. Niko walked up and flashed his employee discount card and scooped up a pair of round ¡BOMBA! cannabis and scorpion tail spherical cigars to accompany the magazines.

The plane took off. Niko sparked up and cracked open the latest issue of SLAM!.

He touched down at 1247pm in Mexico City.

A loud turbine-powered taxicab driven by a coffin of a human being in a black and silver luchador mask shuttled him to his hotel in Los Volcanes.

Over the next few days he drank, smoked fresh Mexico-Exclusive Sol Verde cannabis cigarettes, ate local fare, wore the same clothes, and attended several matches at El Circo, the world-renowned hub of elite lucha libre. The dominating holographic dahlia that adorned the colossal marquee became his favorite artificial sight.

After a satisfying trip to the surprisingly comfortable restroom, Niko was about to scrub away all his theories and questions. All the matches he had watched were lively and clean. The entrances were elaborate and dazzling.

One fellow emerged from the dressing rooms standing tall on the shoulders of an obese silverback gorilla.

He lost.

The one-man-symphony of entrance music was a foul-looking meatball. He sat in the center of an elaborate and confusing array of musical instruments. From his section, Niko could spot several keyboards, an eight-piece drum kit, a trombone, what looked like an accordion on a pedestal, and tabla drums. There was an uncomfortable amount of other items, but he couldn't be sure of all of their exact nature.

Niko chose to pack it in after realizing he had had his fill of acrobatic chicanery. That is, until his keen eyes noticed a familiar looking jobber crying green fluid. The masked man lumbered about the ring like he was lost.

The color of his mask is what gave cause for

alarm. In the brief instant he saw a modicum of green sludge dripping from under his luchador mask, Niko recognized this doddering grappler as the same man he gave the mysterious grunting bag to.

He squinted and tried to be inconspicuous. As soon as Niko could clearly see the source of the fluid, the luchador was surrounded by guards and led away.

Not long after, Niko strolled down the promenade that led away from the thickly-massed arena. Several intricate floral sculptures took turns engaging his interest as he sauntered. Not three blocks away did he pass a local clinic, La Clínica De La Mancha. He stopped walking when he recognized the license plate of an ambulance that had been parked at the El Circo arena lot. He trotted up the door and peeked inside through the glass. There were several people in the lobby; mother's and their children, a sickly looking vagrant, a teenaged couple leaning on each other… nothing atypical to a suburban clinic. Niko turned to leave when he noticed the back entrance, the ambulance port, now had an empty spot. He ducked down the alleyway next to the green-box-of-a-building and peeked around the sudden corner. There, on a gurney, was the same wrestler he had earlier watched be escorted away, the same one he gave the bag to in "Japanese London." He was just lying there, out in the open. Niko assumed the ambulance with a large back door still open to be the one the fellow arrived in. Niko could hear voices floating out from within the building, but they sounded just far enough away for him to steal a few moments with the wrestler. He looked around; no one in the alley, no one walking by on the main drag. Niko crept over to the gurney and poked the man.

Nothing.

He lifted and dropped his arm.

Nothing.

The man felt, not cold, but not warm either. Niko pulled back the sheet draped over the supine luchador and recoiled at the ghastly sight of green slime bubbling forth from a gash in the man's throat. His eyes bulged and stared out at an invisible marvel high in the sky.

Niko knew the story was fact now. The vivid descriptions of the original account nearly sold him upon initial reading, but he just had to see it for himself. When he got back to his hotel room, he tapped into a VPN and trawled for more Mexican zombie stories, only to find an entire web culture built on missing loved ones who had some involvement with El Circo, Sol Verde, and V², El Circo's parent company.

Niko returned, tanned and dusty, to his current home of Darjeeling, a changed man. He would hesitate to call it paranoia, but he had seen behind the curtain and he was not sure how to process what was beheld. He hated the idea of constantly looking over his shoulder or always needing a VPN just to check his fantasy PolyMatic team. Truly, he struggled the most with accepting that such immense and seemingly open lies could exist and proliferate under the protective gaze of the UN.

Niko believed in the UN. His father served in the World Military and his mother was an Ambassador. The rudimentary early school system following the war had done well in completing Niko's education, and the Vocational Training Effort saw to it that he had several journeyman-level trades under his belt, all having been taught concurrently. Because of the UN, he had been able to see the world and work alongside an impossible variety of humans.

All of his recent discovery in Mexico, though, set in stone his disillusionment with the UN, and bolstered his commitment to his Store.

The day he returned, Niko went for a walk in the verdant Sri Gupta Elevated Park and pondered over the way he learned all about Shopping, accepting an anti-UN mindset, and the importance of candor.

Customer Buttcheeks: a peculiar word pairing that would show only every now and then, and only in the deepest parts of the UltraNet.

"Customer *Butt*cheeks?" Niko said the name out loud several times the first time he saw it, really getting the feel of it in his mouth. Information on who, or what, exactly Customer Buttcheeks is, or was, had turned out to be even harder to come by. Some sites said it was a He. Others said a feeling 'from within'.

It was only when he let go of the most

distressing of his thoughts that he noticed a new, unusual, and slightly familiar, storefront near his current job.

"Hey Dev, have you seen that store before?" Niko pointed to the green and gold glass door and fringed awning that was no bigger than a refrigerator.

"Hmm, no. It must be new." Dev replied; his coolness and wan indifference, however, was old hat.

Niko waded through the midday traffic and over to the door. In very small type just above the handle were the letters 'ᗸ' embossed in shimmering gold.

He gently brushed the raised letters with his thumb, which caused an abrupt and jarring buzzing noise. The deep emerald door with intricate bronze Edwardian filigree shook like a gorilla warning an intruder. Passersby reacted with harsh disgust at Niko's attempt at understanding.

Collecting himself, Niko tugged on the handle but nothing happened.

He touched the letters again.

This time, the door popped open.

Before he could enter, a man, bald and pink with a cottony Texas accent poked his head out.

"Son, you're asking to be walked down the aisle into a marriage of pain and suffering. Are we clear?"

"I... I..."

"Boy, I asked you a *question*," the man said. His eyes opened up and he inched out of the doorway a bit more.

In his mind, Niko was poring over the

information he retrieved about Customer Buttcheeks. Not knowing what was false and what was true, he took a shot in the dark.

"The customer is always right!"

"What did you say?" The man's countenance underwent a dramatic change.

"...The customer is always right..." Niko's voice shook. His heart felt like it was pumping out water from a wreck on the Sargasso.

Without another word, the man took Niko's hand and pulled him through the door.

A feeling of diving into a cold lake after spending time in a sauna overtook him. The only other time he felt such a sharp converse of feelings was his trip with his mother to New Thebes while the imposing city was docked in Tokyo.

Everything was dark.

He could still feel the man leading him, but Niko had no idea where.

Now he was sitting.

Without warning, a cover that previously went unnoticed was swiftly removed from his head.

The lights were bright and tinted a sickly green hue.

"What do you know of *The Customer?*" a raspy Manchester voice spoke at him.

"Wha-"

"Silence! Now Speak!"

"Um-"

"He said silence!" A woman's voice. A South Asian flair coated the woman's condemnation.

"Now, tell us what you know of *The Customer!*" A crooked and rusty voice from the rear. Perhaps this person was old, and definitely from somewhere in South America.

Niko wracked his brain and blindly chose another phrase he had come across. "That would be loverly…"

Silence.

Muttering and confluence.

"How long have you been *Ensconced?*" the Desi woman's accusatory voice again.

"What?"

"Silence!"

"He is not *Ensconced*," Pernicious and thick-fingered, Manchester denounced Niko on the spot. A definite thud was felt in Niko's chest on the word 'not'. "He may have trawled for some of the language, but he certainly doesn't *Shop*. There's no way."

"Son, how did you know to touch the letters on the door?" The Texan.

"Lucky guess?"

"Silence!" A *different* woman.

Feeling anxious and a bit guilty about his investigation in Mexico, he chose to volunteer his efforts.

"I recant!" The panic in his voice was real. "It was a mistake to look into Xavier El Burro! I'm sorry, ok!"

Nothing.

Muttering.

"What do you know of *him?*"

"Speak!"

"I… I know about the ooze! Rolando's Tale! I believe it!"

"He knows of the ooze…"

"He knows of the *connection*…"

"Is he clean?"

"The report just came back… yes."

"Nikolaus Ito Sanzenbacher,"

"…Yes?" *How did they get my name?* Niko thought.

"Your actions have rendered you *provisionally acceptable*. How do you respond?"

"I… accept?" Niko had begun to sweat an acrid scent of fear.

"Good. Then I, King Clancy Idyllwild Chesterfield hereby confer upon *you* the rank of Clerk Level I." Having finished speaking, the pink bald Texan then rubbed his mighty hands together and clapped once. The lights in the room shifted and Niko could clearly see there were about seven others in the room with him.

There were schedules on the walls, sales figures, two desks and the lingering smell of refrigerated produce.

"Th-Thank you… I'm sorry but where am I?" Niko asked, at last starting to feel the fear and distrust ebb away.

"Turn around, son."

Niko stood and looked over the several men and women carefully scrutinizing him. Their expressions never wavered. Stone faced and serious, they never took their eyes from him.

Niko slowly turned and noticed a wall of windows overlooking an old American-style grocery store. The aisles were fully stocked and there were both men and women working and shopping.

The Texan came up alongside Niko and placed his heavy catcher's mitt of a hand on his shoulder. "Son, you'll start off by stocking the products. If you do well, you'll man the register. Keep excelling and well... you'll see what's *in store* for you. As for Xavier and his game, you can take heart in the fact that we stand against it."

"Ja, vee do," a Deutsch accent interjected. "I am Viceroy Gudrun Kirshbaum, und in your first assignment, you vill bus *my* table," the tall and leggy brunette winked.

Bussing tables? Niko thought.

"Ya see, there are three core values to being a Customer," the Texan pointed to a large set of words that hung above the entryway and faced inwardly.

"First, we Shop. Then, we Cook. Lastly, we Dine. Shop. Cook. Dine."

"Shop. Cook. Dine." The others in the room all said in unison.

"So... you're all each other's customers?"

"Now you're starting to get it," Manchester said. "The Customer Is Always Right, because the Capitalists *must* be wrong. For too long the human family has suffered at the hands of those who put money before the very people they depend on for survival. The whole 'I need your money, but I definitely don't need you' garbage."

"It's monsters," Viceroy Kirshbaum said. "Like Xavier that forced us to unite in the shadows."

"Ok, so then what power do you, I'm sorry we, actually have?" Niko's appetite was whet.

"You'll learn as you go, just don't go too fast," King Clancy winked and gave him a rough pat on the back.

"Well, now that you're *Ensconced*, your first shift, starting with the Viceroy there, begins in a week. Just come back through the same door in Darjeeling and you'll be met with instructions."

"I vill show you out," Viceroy Kirshbaum walked up and took his hand. Her hand was soft and inviting. This woman obviously took enough time to properly moisturize. The Bavarian goddess led Niko out of the office and down a corridor with freight-packed foodstuffs on one side, and bare wood walls on the other. The cold wet smell of receipt paper, old vegetables, and cleaning supplies wafted in and out of his nose.

"Here, you have to put zis on since you're goink to have to pass srue ze Store itself." She handed him a green vest with an orange and white badge that read 'TRAINEE'.

Niko donned the vest and shook her hand.

"Welcome aboard! And, before I forget, to distinguish *Us* from *Them*, the question is 'Isn't that loverly?' and the answer is 'When the Customer is right...'" She then turned and left.

Niko took a moment to let the rush of the

previous forty-five minutes die down. Once collected, he pushed through the clunky plastic doors and strolled out onto the sales floor.

All around him, every one stopped to look. At least thirty pairs of eyes were now analyzing every inch of his being. From the back, someone called out "He's a trainee!"

Instantly, one by one, all present began smiling and welcoming Niko to the fold.

"Welcome," said a tall flat-chested woman with an apprehensive set of teeth.

"Welcome," this time a short fat Gujarati man smiled and pushed his cart out of the way to bow.

This continued until he had reached the entrance, which was styled after an old movie theater lobby. There, Niko was met by an Usher. The man wore a forest green bellhop's uniform with gold accents. His nametag read Conrad Teague.

"Hello Trainee, where did you come in from?" His transatlantic accent struck Niko as odd, since Niko hadn't heard English so well cared for since his adolescence.

"The new shop in Darjeeling."

"Excellent locale, love the weather. Please step through door 17 as it passes," Conrad Teague stepped back and pulled on a gleaming lever akin to an old ship's speed control.

In front of him an array of bright red velvet curtains were pulled back and a system of doors on conveyor belts was revealed. Each door had a large number painted on it and they shuffled passed him like ducks in a shooting gallery.

"15... 16... ah here we are, door 17."

Conrad Teague now walked over to the door itself and cracked it open.

"The Rosenbridge is ready for pass through, Trainee. Next time you come they'll have a nametag for you. See ya!"

Niko nodded at Conrad and reluctantly stepped over the threshold.

The same flashing hot-to-cold exuberance washed over him and with his next step he fell onto the sidewalk outside the original green and gold door back in Darjeeling. The door snapped shut by itself with a whooshing suction sound behind him.

Niko finished his walk at the exit where several gum trees were arranged in an amorphous colorful interpretation of a long dead empire and checked the time.

1939pm

He broke into a sweaty and panicked run.

Three hours of PolyMatic Football highlights was due on in twenty-one minutes.

2

WEEK 1

LA	V	ESTES
ROME	V	UN
DC	V	LONDON
EDO	V	INCA
SF	V	PARIS
SYDNEY	V	CAIRO
MUNICH	V	BANGKOK
TASHKENT	V	SAIGON
MUMBAI	V	MIAMI
CHICAGO	V	MEXICO
ASSAM	V	MOSCOW
OTTAWA	V	NY

Like sumo, winners in white, losers in black.

The music exploded. Immersive holographics flooded forth from the four-dimensional device and consumed Niko.

"Allllll right! It's Friday at eight of the clock according to UN-Indian-Standardized Time, and THAT. MEANS. FOOTBALL!" Announcer Sanjay Vijay now cranked an old-time fire brigade siren as the graphics danced around a young man in a dingy apartment.

Nikolaus Ito Sanzenbacher leaned back on his favorite wicker and mammoth fur chaise lounger. He crunched on several crisp fried grasshoppers and groped at the low green plaztik table next to his beanbag locus for his bottle of Sri Lankan lager.

"Friends," the dark and severe Bengali said with a clap. "With the exception of today's game, week one has come and gone. Let's get right to it with a recap of one of the more exciting games, The San Francisco Mitsune-gumi Ronin at the Parisian Reign of Terror: SF narrowly overcame Paris and their hi-flying offense with a monster defensive performance when they needed it most…"

The highlight played and Niko reacted to the intricate play the Reign of Terror had tried and failed at running. 1QB Amplified Napoleon Bonaparte, looking very distinguished in his jersey modeled after the monarch's own imperial military garb from over 200 years prior, received the snap. His 2QB, steel-eyed Joachim Murat, took his position seven meters downfield, behind his two tight ends. Napoleon faked a hand-off and chucked the ball to Murat. Murat juggled the catch, but recovered. He too then faked a hand-off to a nearby fullback. He next tried to lateral the ball back to Bonaparte, who was now sprinting along the sideline as the result of a well-executed sweep, when San Francisco 1FS Conrad Atwater jumped the lame-duck pass.

INTERCEPTION!

The purple-haired Oregonian tucked the ball and ran it back to the end zone with less than ten seconds remaining in the game.

TOUCHDOWN!

As the entire defense rallied around the recently-acquired defensive back, Niko thought about how much he really liked the design and color scheme of the San Francisco away uniforms.

The replay jump-cut to a series of shots featuring members of the home crowd reacting with passionate disgust and raw avarice to the tie-breaking score. Atwater's last second takeaway had qualified as a Closing Seconds 10-point Touchdown.

Final score: 43-33, San Fu-Kuo victory.

"The UN won, of course," Sanjay excitedly continued. A quick clip of acrobatic 1QB Bola Nkemediche leaping into the air whilst firing a bullet touchdown pass that wove its way through a triple-team of Roman Legionnaires and into the hands of the league's second leading slot receiver, 3WR Rosamund Rosales of Mindanao.

Final score: 37-25, UN victory.

"A surprisingly absorbing match took place earlier in the heart of the Cybernetic Communist Coalition. Worker's Stadium in Miami was filled to capacity..."

The clip rolled.

The scene opened with Mumbai Federation Of

Scientists 1QB Srinivasa Bose heaving up a prayer as 2DE Clark Stumpf-7J, a Robot and certainly *not* a simulacrum, dragged him to the ground. The ball wobbled its way into the hands of the Miami United Worker's Party ball hawk, 1SS Raul Martinez-Lum.

INTERCEPTION!

The human, clad in the chrome and crimson of the Miami United Worker's Party, ran the ball head on through a mass of convulsing Scientists in their bright cobalt and orange-speckled-black jerseys. The defenseman persisted, spun out of a lame tackle, and flipped into the end zone.

TOUCHDOWN!

"Ouch," Niko said. He briefly remembered the Conference Championship game from three years prior, wherein this same 1QB, Srinivasa Bose, set a record for interceptions thrown in a half.

The next clip from the Mumbai vs. Miami season opener featured the human Miami 1QB, Leonid Kim, call a flea flicker play. The 1RB, a Robot named Vittorio-Bevelacqua-9E, was hit as he turned to pass the ball back to Kim.

FUMBLE!

The ball popped up and over Kim's head, and the race was on. The ball squirted out of the arms of a falling Miami lineman. A Scientist tripped on his own feet and batted the ball with his helmet directly into Kim's hands. The adept Russo-Korean ducked a flying Scientist and whipped the ball to his 2QB, a Robot simply known as Lenin IV.

Lenin IV caught the ball in stride and grabbed a nearby tackle, briefly converting him to a pilot plow.

The 'bot saw the end zone and charged.

TOUCHDOWN!

With less than two minutes in the game, Miami had a two-point lead.

The camera cut to Miami Coach Ineko Asanuma signaling her team to go for two more points, confident that her defense would stand and defend their home field.

The snap.

1QB Leonid Kim executed a perfectly timed play-action fake. 1FB, a Robot, Pavel Tong-5Q slipped out to catch the pass, but it was useless.

The ball was tipped by an alert Scientist, 1CB Anil Bosle.

There was no interception, no return for six; just a smacking sound of the ball bouncing off of the digireal Bermuda grass.

The final clip began with 1QB Bose, a Scientist, flinging the ball like it was a discus, deep down the field. 2WR Ishant Kahn, a tall and incredibly fast Punjabi, had managed to get an arms length away from his pursuant cornerback. The ball suddenly dropped like a plumb weight, a technique known as 'plugging', right into Ishant's hands. The crowd gasped in shock. Ishant took three steps and was drug down from behind. The clock was in the closing seconds, so the ball was rushed to the 30-meter line and spiked.

Soon after, the kicking team was established

and the golden toe of Karishma Kumar-L'Fleur was locked into position.

The snap.

Karishma lined up the ball the instant 2QB Satnam Virk set it in place.

The Mighty Leg of Maharashtra swung.

The ball shot like a champagne cork.

85,000 Miami fans, Robot and human alike, left their home stadium in disappointment.

Final score: 45-44, Mumbai victory.

"She is 31 and 0 in clutch situations," Sachin, Niko's roommate, mentioned through a mouthful of crunchy and spicy fried baby crabs.

"And after a surprise loss by The Gents to the Colonists, 1QB Saxby Lawless had this to say…"

The camera cut to the Edwardian dressing room of the currently featured home team, The London Amplified Gentry. There were white collared shirt-like jerseys in a laundry pile and black tophat-like helmets hanging over each dressing alcove.

The camera was now tight on the face of the franchise. "Y'know, ya can't win 'em all… but let me say this, here and now," the tall blue-eyed-boy-from-the-bayou looked directly into the camera. "I will take this team to the Playoffs, and I will bring the Council Cup to London, one more time," he said with absolute certainty. However, his southern drawl inadvertently made light of his intended seriousness.

The clip ended.

"Well let's hope he can keep his word *this* time," Sanjay added with a cunning look of doubt.

"Yeah," Niko said.

"No kidding…" Sachin remarked, his mouth now half-full with smoky eggplant.

"We can all remember the epic meltdown Lawless had last year after *that* costly interception in OT during one of the more exciting Night Of The High Scores we are able to call to mind…"

The clip rolled.

Statuesque Saxby Lawless dropped back in a traditional, non-PolyMatic, seven-step drop to get some space. When it appeared as if the tall and lanky 3WR Legedu Tsotsi was open, Lawless heaved and reacted with horror as the ball sailed on him and landed right in the hands of the Incan Empire 2CB, Pahuac Quenti. The tattooed and well-spoken Quenti tap danced through several near-miss tackles, but never made it to the end zone. The Incans simply ran out the clock with ground plays and ended the game on a 15-meter chip shot field goal.

While the Obsidian Pumas rejoiced and their fans began to party with less than two minutes left on the clock, Saxby Lawless, a 5-time MVP and 2-time Cup winner, trashed the sidelines. He overturned massage pods, uprooted healing plants, and even injured several interns. After seemingly coming to his senses, Saxby then abruptly left his team and the field. He was found three weeks later on a steamboat in Scotch Vietnam. He was a shell of his normal self. Needless to say, the *hard* partying with his wives and a man claiming to be a missing game show host didn't help his appearance.

"C'mon get to the Proles..." Niko was anxious to experience the coverage of his favorite team.

He had watched the game, which of course was a loss, but re-hashing the highlights always gave him the fix he needed in-between matches.

After a lengthy praising of both the Incan Empire's defensive squad and LA's potential to have a perfect season, Sanjay at last directed his attention to the Have Not division of the League.

"And as for the Have Not's Division, Munich's Meinhardt Vogt Version-VII has come out swinging. Clearly his programming team has done their homework in the off-season. The Meunchen Teutonishen Maschine steamrolled Bangkok, despite an impressive defensive showing at the onset..." Niko marveled at what was being done in Germany as a whole, but the Meinhardt Vogt was a unique treasure in his mind.

Several quick-clips of the prominent green box that was Meinhardt Vogt flashed amidst precision passing and superb tackling from both Munich and the visiting team from Bangkok, The Royal Mass Hysteria

Final score: 38-22, Munich Victory.

"Despite a dazzling and elite performance from 1QB Ferguson Quoc-Duc McPham, most of the Saigon squad had fallen ill by the onset of the 4th quarter, leading to the unusual score shown."

Final score: 60-1, Tashkent victory.

"The normally potent offense just couldn't seem to take advantage of the long bombs and precision passes from the formidable McPham. Not a single player could break the plane." A replay montage rolled with footage of beautiful fundamentals soured by a lack of scoring. The lone rouge earned from a missed Tashkent field goal only made the loss hurt more, one fan was quoted as saying.

"...and in local news, Assam lost, again. Perhaps it's time coach Amjad Tendulkar revisit his rush-centric, option-rooted, offense..."

The highlights came on and Niko shifted to the edge of his seat. The deep red uniforms with illumine snake scales and the black hooded helmets matching a cobra ready to strike gave the Creeping Death all the appearance of a fearsome and worthy opponent. Their play, however, exposed a coach who had no idea what he was doing.

Tendulkar believed solely in the Option Play.

He ate, breathed and slept the option. His 1QB and 2QB, though, had more than a hard time getting around the corner from their respective tackles and guards. Orkis Steptoe, the 1RT was having problems at home that fixed themselves like barnacles to his mind. Meng Zhou Liu, the 1RG had become the victim of powerful hallucinations several years prior after hitting his head during a furiously violent sneezing session at his home. Meng continued trying to play at full tilt, but it was obvious something wasn't right.

The O-line wasn't the only problem though.

The 1QB, Iqbal Kohli, was slow. He won the job over their 2QB, Junichiro Sato, because he was *more* reluctant to throw the ball. Junichiro had a 4.23 40-time, but he loved to hurl the rock, despite how inaccurate he was.

Niko was tired of seeing his team lose. He knew the coach lacked the fortitude to whip his men into shape. But despite the poor execution, he recognized the coach's strategy was overtly the most lethal. Teams like London, Estes Park, Paris, Los Angeles, San Fu-Kuo, etc. all ran West-Coast, pass-heavy, offense. Simply put, they did so because they could afford to. Those larger markets meant larger owners, and with no salary cap, the fields were always white for harvest in the Have Division.

The UN tried to balance out the teams by placing a few token wealthy-market teams in the Have Not division, but those teams just grew into gray whales crammed into kiddie pools.

Niko raised his eyes to his most sacred piece of Assam Creeping Death memorabilia: a framed, signed, game-worn, Bud Grimsby jersey sporting his unique number, *99*. Bud was the only halfback allowed to wear the number typically reserved for 1QBs and defensive linemen. Each time Niko looked at the shimmering black and red uniform, he was reminded of exactly how Bud Grimsby had earned the letter from the Lord Commissioner allowing him to bear the two nines with pride.

THE LEGEND OF BUD GRIMSBY

Assam Creeping Death at Sydney Copper Locusts.

14 December 2151.

The Sikkimese Rhino Formation

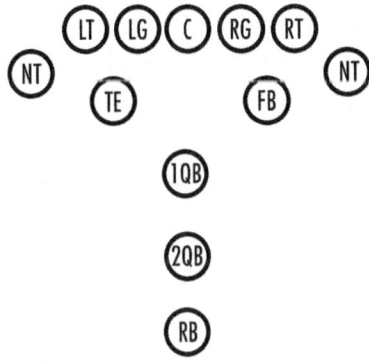

It was second down with four yards to a fresh set.

1QB Iqbal Kohli broke the huddle and trotted to his position at the helm of the Sikkimese Rhino formation.

The sun made the white scales on the Assamese team's away jerseys glimmer with a rainbow sheen.

Kohli did his best to read the tricky Sydney

defense. Beyond his wall of guards and tackles was a copper sea of ravenous Locusts.

At his flanks were Basu and Mbatha: his fullback and tight end, respectively. 1TE Praxad Mbatha flexed her fingers in anticipation of the snap. Behind Kohli, rookie 1RB Bud Grimsby, all 165 centimeters of him, stood at the ready. He wore number *14*; a carryover from his stellar career at his alma mater.

Kohli's cadences fell like dinner plates. His throat cracked and warbled as he tried to bark out protection adjustments.

His voice quivering, Kohli called the snap.

The line slid right.

Kohli bobbled the snap.

The ball ricocheted from his left palm and wobbled through the air right into Bud's waiting arms.

He followed his blocks.

1FB Ashok Basu pancaked a blitzing 1FS Rory Phipps, creating a brief alcove for Grimsby to slip through.

He weaved around two grappling players and punched a hole through the secondary.

All he could see was end zone.

He picked up his pace and pumped his stubby legs with furiousness.

Suddenly, the overlooked 1SS Sekope Timani could be seen cutting in at a sharp diagonal. He was running downhill at full speed, straight at Grimsby. The man's billowing mane made him appear like a starved and hunched beast primed to strike at its first meal in ages. Timani's copper orange and lime green jersey with blue and platinum accents seemed to amplify his imposing rush.

I thought I was through… Bud said to himself.

He switched carrying arms.

Timani timed his breathing and braced for a crushing tackle.

Grimsby feigned ignorance.

Timani leapt to spear his prey. His facemask was met with the hardest stiff-arm he had ever encountered at that point in his career. The highlight from that legal football maneuver would go on to become part of the PolyMatic football legend.

The defender's body crumpled into itself for a brief instant before twisting up, around, and completely out of the way of the passing Grimsby.

The Assamese fans sprinkled amongst the home Australian crowd exploded in jubilation.

Grimsby flew down the field, now truly unchallenged.

TOUCHDOWN!

When all was said and done in that particular round, Grimsby had repaired a busted play, broken three tackles, obliterated a storied and proud defenseman, and ultimately scampered eighty-two meters for the score.

After that performance, Grimsby had the hot hand. Head Coach Tendulkar breathed a visible sigh of relief. He could taste his feverish addiction to the option play was finally going to pay some dividends. *And all this against a team from the Have's Division to boot!*

The tall but dour Indian thought to himself.

For the rest of the game, Bud Grimsby took eighty percent of the snaps.

Hike.

Ball.

Go!

However, Sydney would not go down quietly on their home field.

1QB Stanley Porter Livingston responded to the frenzied ground attack by unleashing his own raging aerial bombardment of the Assamese defense. For five straight possessions the team wearing glossy green helmets with shimmering copper decals of compound eyes did the two things locusts excel at: eating and flying. The Locusts ate meter after meter of field. The ball was caught and advanced by all three starting receivers, both tight ends, both running backs, a fullback, and even a pair of tackles caught an end zone bomb and a 20-meter lob respectively.

Sydney kept up the assault for the entire second half, but Grimsby couldn't be stopped.

In the fourth quarter, Coach Tendulkar began swapping his Nose Tackles for Wide Receivers, as well as placing Grimsby in on kick return.

He scored twice on kickoffs.

Livingston now started keeping the ball longer and moving it downfield personally. He didn't trust his 2QB, Neville Namatjira, to properly assist him in this battle. That's not to say they weren't a cohesive unit, Livingston just knew that today was not his partner's day. Livingston would score again and again, keeping the Creeping Death no more than one score behind.

On the next Assam possession, 2RT Ming Zhou Liu sprang into action after the snap on first down. He created a crease for Grimsby to pass by, but as the tiny baller flew passed him, Ming hallucinated a fissure in the earth. He began screaming with a forceful vibrato. He genuinely feared for his teammates' safety. The play ended with a seven-meter gain, but Ming had to be forcibly put into a healing pod. He would miss the remainder of the game.

Without Ming to lead the charge, Kohli became a nervous wreck. Head coach Tendulkar subsequently elected his 2QB to switch with Kohli and become the Prime.

Junichiro Sato and his infamous facial scar stepped into position behind the line.

Instead of the Rhino, Sato called an audible: Shotgun spread with an empty backfield.

Grimsby lined up in the slot position.

Sato gave a hard count and got 210 kilo 2NT Tom Howard to jump into the neutral zone.

Sato confidently led the men and women around him to the new primary line of scrimmage. His keen eyes then honed in on a shaky-looking defender.

Utilizing the no-huddle approach, Sato called out the desired play in code: Sluggo 12, Y 5, Z GO, *Sharp knife, sharp knife,* break!"

The squad deployed with Kohli taking Sato's traditional spot on the weak side behind Mbatha the tight end.

Just before he gave the signal to go, Sato called out one last adjustment: "KILL, KILL! APE SWEAT! APE SWEAT! APE SWEAT!" Sato flapped his arms and bore his teeth.

A quick reorganization moved Grimsby from Sato's left to his right, and 1WR Hardeep Tanaka shifted to the slot.

The snap.

As the ball traveled from Center to Quarterback, Sato noticed the game clock. This was most likely going to be the possession that determines the game's outcome. This brief flash of realization caused him to bobble the snap. The ball's wild movements stole his attention, thus creating an opportunity for blitzing linebacker Sukarno Lesmana. Somehow, Sato was able to corral the ball and slip through Lesmana's wrap-and-twist. He took three wobbly steps on his tiptoes before flinging the ball into a cluster of white, red, copper, and green.

INTERCEPTION!

1MLB Cedric Ghoulsby plucked the ball from the air and began his downhill campaign.

"JAILBREAK! JAILBREAK!" The colossal man called as his fellow defensemen rallied around in escort.

Well, Bud Grimsby was not about to just take the turnover without a fight. Using his small stature, he blended in amongst the throng of players in pursuit of the ball.

The convoy crossed the Center Line and continued its hulking progress.

72

A window opened.

Bud shot in, and with his helmet, he dislodged the ball.

FUMBLE!

The fastest man on the Assamese offense, before the emergence of Bud Grimsby, was the lanky and well-read 1WR Hardeep Tanaka. The sharp-eyed and red-bearded athlete scooped up the wobbling Nabob and took off for the end zone. The defenders were closing in, but Tanaka knew the game couldn't end on a field goal. It was simply against the rules.

Tanaka cut across the field after moving the ball passed the Center Line.

Shortly after, at the Sydney 25 meter line, Tanaka was brought down by an exhausted 3CB, Wallis Kelly.

1:47 remains in the 4th quarter.

Assam reassembled the Rhino.

The snap.

Sato fed Grimbsy.

Grimsby ran for 10 meters.

No huddle.

1:29 left.

The snap.

Grimsby, fed.

10 more meters in his wake.

No huddle.

1:08 left.

The snap.

Grimsby fakes on Play Action.

Sato floats the ball to Mbatha, who is tackled at

the two-meter line.

Sydney calls timeout.

47 seconds remain.

When play resumed, Sydney sent out its heavy goal line package: four nose tackles, five linebackers, and three safeties.

Tendulkar responded by sending out two of his nose tackles in place of tight ends.

Sato received the call from the sidelines: Staggering drunk with a liquid possum, on two.

The Obese Quadruped formation was complete. Five o-line men, the two nose tackles on the flanks, the two fullbacks doubled-up behind them, Sato behind the center, Grimsby behind him, and Tanaka split out wide.

Men and women on both sides of the ball shot burning stares at their counterparts.

The snap.

The o-line collapsed.

The large and angry defensemen invaded the backfield.

Before Sato was down, the ball traversed the air between him and Grimsby with deft fluidity.

Grimsby spun out of a tackle and broke into a lateral run.

"No! NORTH! GO NORTH!" Tendulkar shrieked from the sideline.

Like the heads of a hydra the Sydney players

kept appearing from behind the line; Grimsby couldn't find the edge and turn the corner.

The sideline was quickly approaching. Realizing this, Grimsby planted his left hoof and turned back, cutting directly against a hard wave of momentum.

He lunged awkwardly towards the goal line, but was met by a Locust. Bud bounced off of the defender and was sandwiched into another. The jarring sensation of ricocheting between two humongous players sent Grimsby northward at last.

Without immediately realizing it, the Locusts had pinballed Grimsby in for the tying, Closing Ten-Seconds, ten-point score.

TOUCHDOWN!

Tendulkar was incredulous.

The small but raucous visiting troupe of fans erupted in celebration. This was the best their team had done against the Aussies in over a decade.

Tendulkar sent out his ace kicker for the extra, game winning, point. The one thing no one faulted the Creeping Death for was their kicker, Priyadarshini Patel. She wore her 94% success rate as a badge of honor. The fans wore her jersey, number *11*, with the same pride.

She plucked several blades of grass to check the wind at field-level. The streamers atop the goal posts signified no cross-breeze. She gave her signal.

The snap.

The kick.

2DE Bronwyn Unaipon got his telescopic arms up just in time.

The ball made a crushing thud as it wanly bounced off of the defenders finger tips.

The holder, Himesh the Punter, proved to be the spryest player in range and threw himself onto the live ball.

This was the end of regulation time.

Assam won the coin toss.

The Meter-Wheel was spun.

It landed on -20 SYDNEY.

Their No-Field-Goal-Sudden-Death campaign would begin in the Copper Locust Red Zone.

Iqbal Kohli managed to coerce Tendulkar to switch him and Sato once more, restoring the order shown on the depth chart.

From the Rhino, called by Tendulkar of course, Kohli audibled into a modified Pistol with a Double-Stack of receivers, Grimsby being one of them. Next to him, where Bud would usually stand at the ready, was Praxad Mbatha. The Lioness, as she is known, rested her hands on her knees in the ready position.

The snap.

Grimsby ran the prescribed sluggo route and executed the false comeback with elite precision. The defense bit and two CB's fell to the earth.

Mbatha picked up the Safety blitz but lost her footing after a clump of linemen were forced into her path. 200 kilo Tom Howard, still mad about the neutral zone infraction from earlier, hurled his blockers to the ground and flung his girth at Kohli. The force of the blow sent the ball sailing into the air towards the middle of the field.

Bud Grimsby plucked the unusual pass from the air in stride and bolted for home.

The last Sydney player in range forced every drop of his energy into his legs. He had started near the goal line, but like the rest of the defense, he fully invested in the fake slant. The best he could do now was a shoestring tackle at an angle that could've injured both of them.

He went for it.

The defender lunged for Bud's rapid-fire legs.

Bud saw the man and timed his actions. He cut to his right at the 3-meter marker and suddenly took to the air, back first.

TOUCHDOWN!
GAME OVER.

Victory, Assam Creeping Death.

The clip of the graceless 240° turn Grimsby made in the air as the defender fell in a failed tackling motion was the highlight of the week.

Thus the legend was born.

The letter from the High Commissioner, granting Grimsby the right to wear his now-infamous *99* arrived the day before their next game.

From that game on, Bud Grimsby was the centerpiece of the Assam Creeping Death's increasingly fearful ground attack.

"**...S**o what do you think Lamont? Can Coach Clancy take The Firm to 20-0?" Sanjay Vijay asked one of his staple panel members, retired HOF* 1QB Lamont Drexler.

"Oh Sanjay, something tells me Clancy Chesterfield has more than a few tricks up his sleeve, and after the way the defense came through and delivered for him on Sunday, I think we're going to be looking at a loverly- I mean lovely! A *lovely* season." Lamont Drexler hastily smiled a nervous, toothy grin. The gesture was delivered the same way a towel would be when catching someone fresh out of the shower. A single bead of sweat broke from its cell on his shiny black forehead and bolted down his right cheek.

"Did he just say..." Niko thought he misheard the enormous black man. This single Freudian slip on behalf of the storied player planted a seed in Niko.

If Xavier and his entire operation in Mexico is sanctioned by the UN, who's to say The League isn't at least as corrupt?

Niko leapt up from his beanbag chair and went to his balcony-mounted collection of narcoplants. He needed mental clarity for the task at hand, so he snipped off a cluster of foxtail amphorchid and brought it in for preparation. He laid the luminous pink and white flower mass onto his bamboo cutting board and manually picked off several opened buds. He swiftly popped two directly into his mouth and put

78

on a kettle to boil with the rest inside.

Right away he felt the boost from the two buds already eaten. He took out his computer and took a deep breath. Niko was about to investigate the reality of his most favorite thing in the world. His trip to *Hall Of Fame Mexico had yielded valuable, horrifying, information. Had everything he'd watched been a lie? Were there *any* genuine competitions left in the UN's world?

"Look, man, wrestling has always been fake. Well, at least until Xavier showed up. But regardless, The League *is* real. Just accept it," Sachin Tiwary, Niko's closest friend and roommate, was trying to dissuade any and all investigations into The Most Beautiful Game.

"Besides, how do you know that looking into these things wont come back and bite you, eh? As far as I am concerned, when I watch the *Death*, I am watching pure sport."

Niko adjusted his apron and regarded his friend with intellectual suspicion. Sachin worked at a local TASC annex as a statistical probability analyst, so Niko knew his friend was intelligent. He also knew his friend was a bit strange. At last three times a week, Sachin would head out to the lowest reviewed restaurants and order the most hated dishes. Sachin said he did it as a bit of an existential proof, and a little bit because he made it a point to enjoy things other people actively hated. What Niko feared was Sachin looking for ways to lie to himself about the world around him. Everyone craves stability and wants to believe the world that's presented to them; but only the truly foolish dive in without question.

"You really think a group of people would leave a $100,000,000,000GD industry up to chance?" Niko proposed.

Sachin never had a snappy, deeply-held comeback for that one.

As the regularly timed commuter train lumbered past his window, Niko wondered how long it would be until he was in the Kitchens at The Store. As a boy, his mother had occasionally taught him how to prepare several local and foreign dishes, in between UN sessions. His favorite by far was his personal take on Baingan Bhurta, an exquisite smoky eggplant dish from the Punjab.

Niko extended his arm and reached for the sizzling whole eggplants that were on his balcony-mounted grill. The white cedar charcoal his mother sent him from Aomori gave the eggplant a haunting crispness that subtly cut through the creamy dish but did not steal the spotlight. The charcoal, when combined with mesquite chips, made for a perfect smoking medium.

"Hey it's starting!" Sachin called to Niko who was moving another batch of eggplant from his grill to his food-mangler.

"I'm coming!" Niko called back in through their screen door.

Niko eventually got settled in his mammoth chaise, while Sachin stretched his long legs on the hideous yellow couch the two had found in the lobby.

Luther Lane and Jean-Yves Martel were now filling the entirety of the holovision.

"Hello, Bonjour, and Konichiwa to the world as we get set for Wednesday Night Football."

3

"It is exactly 0015 in the AM here in the Capitalist Empire of Los Angeles, Jean-Yves, what are you looking forward to tonight?"

Luther "Brick" Lane, a bombastic former 1CB who played for London, always regarded his broadcasting teammate in Jean-Yves as a pirate-faced man with bulbous, chameleon-like, eyes that truly reminded him of a beloved actor of his, Marty Feldman. In the several microseconds that passed after his question to the Frenchman, Luther toiled at suppressing his urge to malform his facial expression in revulsion.

The proud man both from Brittany and several successful Parisian Reign of Terror squads oscillated his spheroidal eyes towards their mutually captive audience. "Tonight Bwicke, I am very much zo looking forward to watching those crafty and dangerous Twins from Estes Park and zeeing what gadget plays they will have to employ against Clancy's team."

"Yeah, y'know the last time these two teams played each other, we ended up in triple OT."

"Oh oui, ze infamous 'All-Nighter'" Jean-Yves intoned before cutting into the pan-seared foie gras with Gewurztraminer gelee and pickled winesap apples that sat before him.

"You'd think that since they're in the same division, there'd be a *modicum* of understanding." Brick Lane winked at the camera before stirring his bowl of bhindi masala, prawn curry, and paella.

"Indeed, one would eggspect zat."

"Regardless, there's certainly no love lost between these two, right Jean-Yves?"

"None whatsoever, Bwicke."

"Looks like the teams have limbered up and taken their supplements. Let's throw it down to Ines da Silva on the sidelines…"

The camera wiped away from the lush broadcasting booth and its two beguiling occupants in gaudy suits to a robust and effervescent aqua-haired woman with a sparkling pink microphone.

She stood on the visiting Estes Park sideline in a matching pink pencil skirt and peacock sport coat. Her electric green eyes dominated her face and her cornflower blue lips oozed an invisible attention stealing honey. The woman could embarrass a host of men when it came to her encyclopedic knowledge of the sport and its history. This, along with her most pointed way of speaking, kept the focus on her face, and not on her generous bosom. The engrossingly reflective gold heels, open-toed to display her perfect pedicure, lifted her buttocks into an almost pointed shape. Most of the senior players took her visit in stride, while many of the rookies simply froze in place, their eyes welded to the fountain of light reflecting from her passing elegance. The female players shook their heads and laughed while they waited for their turn at getting to ogle the Adonis sideline reporter currently causing rookie fainting episodes along the LA home bench.

The Estes Park Ubiquitous Simulacra bench traveled well, albeit rather heavily: Massage tables, water-producing mangroves, Amplified gardens (all teams head these on their sidelines), a WAG section, a pop-up kitchen, and two healing pods.

The LA home side had generally the same stuff that Estes Park had brought, but the home team's amenities were stadium fixtures and thus not subject to the wear-and-tear of road games.

"Thanks, *boys*... and I'm *not* being facetious!"

The camera widened out to show this week's *Saboteur*: local girl Lindsey Welles from Silverlake. The angular nose and mousy face of blonde Lindsey Welles lit up as she began jumping to show her excitement.

"SPIN! SPIN! SPIN!" roared the crowd.

Ines da Silva simply smiled and guided her audience to behold the Wheel of Enrichment. What was interesting, though, was that, the Wheel of Enrichment wasn't so much of a wheel, as it was nearly impossible to fathom grid-like network of possibilities. There was no end to the combination of upgrades and downgrades that the Saboteur, chosen via lottery each week, got to randomly select from.

The only part that qualified the 'Wheel' portion of the Wheel of Enrichment was the only thing that the Saboteur physically engaged.

Lindsey, sporting an ear-splitting smile, gripped the 'wheel' toggle and gave it a surprising spin.

At once the probability matrix became active. The customary Cube Entity formed; a loosely held together magnetic field that served as the output monitor for the quantum dodeco-core processing engine built into the platform. The Cube rattled and made its customary sound of a maelstrom approaching its zenith. The crowd watched in fervent anticipation of the machine's chosen Enrichment for their viewing.

All at once the lights in the arena went out.

Not one second later, they were back on.

The Cube Entity solidified its decision for all to see.

"3RD DOWN? HANDEGG RULES! A.S."

"Now here's an interesting Enrichment!" Brick Lane was outwardly pleased with the Wheel of Enrichment's ruling.

An explanatory clip was queued, and then played.

"The A.S., or *All Squads*, at the end means this Enrichment applies equally to both teams, for the entire game." A Canadian referee appeared onscreen and proceeded to demonstrate what was said.

"When the Offense reaches 3rd Down, all pre-snap actions, passing actions, and running actions will be judged according to the rules of PolyMatic

Football's predecessor, Traditional Football, or what is today known as HandEgg."

The cacophonous and bass-heavy foghorn sounded, indicating it was time for the coin toss. The Wheel of Enrichment was shuttled away by its handlers. Lindsey Welles followed Ines to the Lounge area, leaving a trail of drooling, but not leering, admirers.

Captains from both sides trotted out to the Center Line. For Estes Park, it was the cunning and focused Jemineye twins, their 1TE Ingmar Shockey, and their red-headed kicker Peg 'The Leg' Chamoix. The Los Angeles Firm of Payne, Suffering, and Pheir, commonly known as The Firm, sent out their cocky and brash 1QB Blackburn Fitzpatrick, their powerful and unmatched 1RB Kingdom Foxx, and their fearsome 2DE Lawrence Awl.

Chief Referee Manfred Feldspar, fresh from a perfectly scored season, held out the BankParlous-sponsored coin.

"Heads is the UN Seal, tails is the Season Identifier," the short and pudgy black man said.

The coin went up, and Larry Awl called out "Tails!"

It landed face up.

"We'll receive," Cassandra barked, locking her explosively green and pixelated helmet on. The six-foot-four star then turned and trotted to the sideline with her identical twin sister in tow.

Helga and Cassandra Jeminye were arguably the most intimidating athletes in The League. The meters they put up throwing and scrambling as individuals in a single game were often times more than the entire opposing team's effort. If you made the mistake of intercepting a pass, one of them *will* tackle you, and it *will* hurt. Their cadence was deep and fierce. They were key players on the first and only back-to-back-to-back Council Cup team. Their discriminating, analytical, eyes could cause a defense to collapse on an atomic level. On top of that, the pair were renowned, statuesque, and unrivaled beauties. Their wavy blonde locks tumbled forth from beneath their helmets. Their blinding white teeth illuminated any room they entered. There were entire gossip columns and blogs dedicated to the immense size and captivating sharpness of their noses. Cassandra had eyes that most sports writers described as "the closest thing to seeing the crab nebula in person." Helga's violet irises reminded several close associates of amethyst geodes under a spotlight.

Helga spoke each of the Seven UN Standard languages fluently. Cassandra was a shrewd and eloquent property owner. Helga organized community hydroponic gardening in the off-season. Cassandra owned a HATEBAKE franchise on Big Thompson Avenue and would often work in the adjacent café during her offseason.

The gorgeous elite athletic champions also just so happened to be Estes Park locals. Their parents had moved to Estes Park to work in the emerging field of recreational simulacra. Unbeknownst to Bertram and Melita Jeminye, though, the couple was pregnant. Melita chose to continue working throughout her pregnancy after finding out. With the help of several Amplified botanicals, she was able to easily and readily contribute to the work.

After the twins were born, their parents made them as much a part of the work as they themselves were involved. The girls grew up playing with hypereal appendages and rudimentary AI half-humans as toys.

In fact, it was the twins' love for the PolyMatic game that led to their parents developing simulacra that could participate in sporting events without having an advantage over a human competitor. A finely balanced AI sentience combined with body parts that can pop off instead of break and patented liquid circuitry served as the perfect cocktail for the first generation of athletic simulacra. By the time the twins were ready to go pro the simulacra had been perfected.

Having unanimously won the Smengler-Jyx trophy in college, the twins were able to cherry pick their home team and ink a secret deal prior to going number 1 as a duo overall in the draft.

The reflective deep green 2D8000 base, layered with an ascending, sparkling, pixelated green gradation of 3AA401 to 4ED109 to 8CE45D comprised the pattern of the Estes Park home uniform that made the powerful women appear as though they were engulfed in a chartreuse inferno.

The goddesses strode up and down the lavish away-team sideline, rousing their teammates, those of flesh and those hypereal, to action.

Niko and Sachin readjusted themselves and double-checked their snack supply and beer levels.

The spider camera rotated to a position behind the LA kicker, Carmen Finster, and captured every second of her tremendous wind up and delivery.

The stone gray (6F746C and 454943), digicam patterned gravelgrip Nabob ball with electric lime green (58FE00) laces sailed end-over-end into the hands of the eager Estes Park Special Teams ace, Germaine Pax, who speedily brought the ball out from the end zone.

"Risky choice, but if anyone is going to try it…" Luther expertly called the game in between bites of food.

Pax cut a few times, causing several defenders to miss. The crowd's noise-level grew with each meter the small and nimble man put in his rearview. After a precarious spin move, there was only the kicker to beat.

Number *17* locked eyes with her and charged forward. Carmen Finster strafed just long enough to make a dive for his ankles. Her right index finger caught just enough of Pax's shoelace to add a slight stutter to his step. The man soldiered on, but his painful attempts to stay upright only carried him as far as the 15-meter line. Still, the Jeminye twins were noticeably happy to start with a short field.

Deploying in a Traditional Estes formation, with five offensive linemen, two tight ends, one fullback, one half back, and one wide receiver, Cassandra took her spot in the shotgun while Helga lined up behind the 1TE.

Cassandra read the defense: she could tell the NT's were rushing, as usual, the DE's may be looking to go out into coverage, the OLB's are disguising a blitz, the ILB's are splitting coverage and blitzing, and the Secondary is playing close to the numbers.

Noticing the impending collapse, Cassandra decided to call out an audible for a quick slant pass to Helga, with the possibility of another strike to their 2WR Xi Zhou Dao, the small but formidable slot receiver from Hubei.

Cassandra quieted the over-capacity crowd, affording all in attendance a chance to hear her famous cadence.

"*Uncle*... Unnncle Susan..."

The tackles each repositioned in an almost imperceptible fashion.

"Hut... *hut!*"

The D-line blinked.

"MARTHA! MARTHA! *Powderdry!*"

Cassandra darted her piercing daggers while opening and closing her hands, simultaneously rotating her upper torso from side to side, clicking her tongue in-between howls of "Powderdry... Powderdry..."

The snap.

The collapse occurred.

1RB Finley Allen Doyle, a simulacrum, picked up the blitz.

Helga opened up.

Cassandra ducked a flying Larry Awl and fired

the pass in her trademark, full-voiced, gladiator-with-a-spear style.

"C'mon!" She wailed as the synthetic oblong totem exploded from her grip.

Helga caught the bullet in stride and pushed her lone simulacrum tight end downfield five meters and then saw Dao's number *81*.

Helga completed her prerequisite plant, locked her purple beholders onto the proficient teammate, and fired an odd shovel pass to Dao. The ball wove its way through the arms of a nearby defender, but was tipped off the helmet of a different falling defender.

Dao climbed up and over his pesky CB to snatch the ball from *his* intercepting hands. The ensuing mid-air struggle of 0.45 seconds resulted in Dao's falling into the End Zone, 3CB Andy Sherman in defeated tow.

"Whoa..." both men watching at home in Darjeeling let out.

"...And just like that, Estes Park is on the board!" Luther jovially proclaimed. The room filled with green-drenched pixelated graphics to celebrate the Estes Park score.

"Well with a 95 meter return to start the show..." Even Jean-Yves was impressed with the lightning speed displayed.

On the LA sideline, Coach Clancy Chesterfield applauded his defense. He knew the Jemineye twins were a force, but he also knew their proclivity to start strong but fade out around the start of the 4th quarter. Through his thin-slit eyes he was watching the girls bounce and cheer their brief victory.

"Fitzpatrick!" King Clancy called out.

"Yes, coach?" The Herculean 1QB trotted up beside the team's unquestioned leader.

"Remember that play we talked about in camp, the *Salnicker-Raskol*?"

"Yes, sir."

"Let's start with that."

"…And at the start of the 4th quarter, we are looking at a score of 40 to 17 in favor of Estes Park."

"Yes, Luter, this has been an eggciting matchup. That Closing Seconds Field Goal in the first half really helped to push Estes Park over LA."

"No kidding, and what about that False Start HandEgg call in the 2nd that cost LA their position in the Red Zone?"

"You know Luter, I used to be a betting man, but the frustrations of HandEgg rules and its bureaucracy drove me away," the Frenchman gave a dramatic gesture of expulsion. "I had hoped Coach Clancy's squadron would 'ave… been better prepared for such an Enrichment."

"But, the game's not over folks, in fact, some say that the 4th quarter is when true PolyMatic football is played…"

The final quarter began with Cassandra Jemineye targeting her newly-acquired 1WR, Mr.

Moss, three times in a row. The way she would employ the read-option when an opposing team was on the ropes had begun to be taught in schools across the globe. However, as she looked for her towering receiver's open hands over a sea of carnage for the fourth time, the ever-hawkish 1FS Leveon DuBois caught the pass after it was tipped by none other than Larry Awl. Cassandra herself flew into a rage and chased the man down, almost stripping the ball from his copper arms. The sideline towel and water boys quaked in their athletic shoes as Cassandra and Helga stormed to their bench.

"Told ya..." King Clancy said as Blackburn Fitzpatrick jogged passed him and out onto the field.

But after a long drive from one 20-meter line to the other, The Firm had to finally settle for a field goal.

40-20, Estes Park.

With the ball back, Estes Park brought out a few of their more exotic plays: a no-pass option frenzy for one series that led to a punt, a turn for Helga at the 1QB position that also led to a punt, and a blocked Field Goal attempt that led to three points for The Firm.

40-23, Estes Park.

Time was winding down, and King Clancy was starting to get agitated.

"Ok now Blackie, *I need you to calm down*, I see what they're doing on that field just like you do. You want that perfect season don't you?" the solid man did his best to fortify and stabilize his 1QB.

"Coach, it's that Psycho look! I won't deal with a line that can't keep the Safeties out of my face, and I can't throw to people that won't at least push off every now and then! I mean, a *Nose Tackle* covering a *Tight End?* By the time Shapiro gets into position, Maddox or Kringle or one of 'em is trying to drown me!" The normally cool hurler was quickly unraveling.

Clancy took the onslaught of emotion in stride. As soon as Fitzpatrick had finished speaking, Clancy grabbed his shoulders and looked him square in his deep azure eyes.

"Look, son, you don't have a choice. We *need* that Multi-Man Bonus Chip for the big dance, and you're going to get it for *me*..."

'For me'? Fitzpatrick thought. It was unusual for the coach to inject his personal concerns into a game. Clancy was known for building up the team with nearly every word spoken.

Fitzpatrick nodded and tried to not display his curiosity in the coach's new word choice.

"Good, good. Now head out there and get us 7 points closer to that 20 & 0," King Clancy winked and rotated his headset mic back to in front of his thin-lipped mouth.

The quarterback locked his helmet on and waited for the Meter-Wheel to determine where the next series would start.

The offensive line broke from the huddle first and got set on the 40-meter line on the LA side.

Fitzpatrick motioned his two tight ends to the strong side, then had his 1 and 2 receivers enter the backfield. His hard-nosed running back Kingdom Foxx split out wide next to the 2QB E.G. Shapiro.

He read the defense, as best he could, but given what has been happening all day, Fitzpatrick had no idea what to expect.

The snap.

Fitzpatrick dropped back deeper from his shotgun position and handed the ball off to Kingdom Foxx on a sweep.

Foxx trotted forward, waiting for a hole open.

The tight ends broke from their blocks and began their push up field.

Foxx saw a hole develop and took his shot for a great 12-meter pickup.

The line reset and Fitzpatrick called out the play, utilizing the no-huddle method.

The snap.

Fitzpatrick ducked a blitzing cornerback and took off, seeing no one was open downfield, and made it 5 meters before sliding.

Quickly, Fitzpatrick called out another no-huddle quick pass to get the first down.

The snap.

The slot receiver Demetrius Shaw came open after ILB Terrence Fillian dove for Foxx on a fake.

Shaw caught the pass and spun out of a diving tackle from safety Porter Stork. From there, he wove his way through the traffic and gained another ten meters.

Fitzpatrick barked out yet another no-huddle play and scrambled to the line, at last in Estes Park territory.

On the sidelines, Helga Jeminye mimed out plays to the secondary, while Coach Iggy Chisholm made hand signals for the D-line.

The snap.

The two tight ends met up on the weak side of the field after three or so meters just as Shapiro found himself directly behind them.

Fitzpatrick side-armed the ball to Shapiro, who then planted and fired to 2WR Keyshawn Mingo down field.

The ball was caught, and the spindly Keyshawn took off laterally to get some space, only to feel the mighty crunch of Larry Awl who had peeled off into coverage along the strong side.

With the ball at the 15-meter line, King Clancy took his penultimate timeout.

Fitzpatrick, Shapiro, Foxx, and their tight ends finished their Amplified mangrove water, chewed on some Erythroxylum-Ilex hybrid leaves, and locked their helmets back on.

As the teams took the field, the defense came out in the Psycho defensive formation that Fitzpatrick had come to abhor: 1 down lineman, Safeties on Receivers, and a bunch of upright wandering giants, none making eye contact with Fitzpatrick.

The offense lined up for a slobber-knocking

bulldozer play: Fitzpatrick would snap the ball from the gun amidst a tightly knit O-line supporting an empty backfield and then start plowing ahead as blockers would peel off and pour in ahead of him from the wings.

The snap.

The line roared to life, pushing back the five blitzers. The tight ends peeled off from their blocks and dove inwards, towards the center of the fleshmass. The receivers were next, bending back the heaving wall. Finally, Fitzpatrick himself tucked the ball into his midsection and engaged his quadriceps. The ten-meter line came and went, followed by the five.

Fitzpatrick grit his teeth and spied the goal line. Just as he moved to score, an unexpected and punishing hit from Larry Awl jarred the ball loose.

The stout and scrappy Kingdom Foxx was put in place as the tail end of the bulldozer for instances such as this.

Without losing his stride, Foxx plucked the ball from the hearty fescue after one bounce, and took to the air.

The small man soared over the mass of male and female professional athletes, landing heartily on his padded rear in the End Zone.

40-29, Estes Park w

3:31 minutes remain on the clock.

On the sideline, King Clancy held up two fingers, letting the offense know that they needn't leave the field.

The O-line got in place, bolstered by the tight ends and the receivers, all packed closely together. Fitzpatrick was the dot of the Pistol-based I-formation they had planned to run the play from. Behind him were the legendary Fullback, Regina Alstott, and of course, Kingdom Foxx.

The snap.

The entirety of the offense above Fitzpatrick rolled hard to the left, weak side, while Regina Alstott snuck out to the right, strong, side and caught the delicate butterfly of a pass, trotting merrily, untouched, into the end zone. Her hearty spike and gripping dance thereafter served as a perfect exclamation point to her first score of the season.

40-31, Estes Park

3:26 to go.

The needle of the Meter Wheel landed on the 35-meter line of Estes Park, so inevitably both sides jogged out to that point on the field.

Cassandra didn't bother reading the defense, given the score and time remaining, and elected to eat as much clock as she could.

A hand-off for three meters.

Another, yet poorly disguised, hand-off for three more.

Cassandra dropped back to pass from under center, and instead ran a delayed sweep, but 1RB Finley Allen Doyle bobbled the exchange and put the ball on the ground.

FUMBLE!

The LA man known as the Minotaur, white

haired Maori 2DE Declan Ngata, broke his block and scooped up the ball, knocking Finley Allen Doyle out of his way.

Estes Park speedo model and 2TE Cenk Suleiman, a simulacrum, ran down Ngata and collided with him at the 15, losing an arm in the process.

Immediately the offense sprinted onto the field, the replay still demolishing the fan's hopes for a decisive win.

Fitzpatrick split Shapiro out wide, and called his 1TE Orville Skinner to block on the weak side.

The snap.

Skinner picked up the blitzing safety, and Shapiro got open behind the other tight end, Wang Hongwen. Fitzpatrick took his shot, hitting Shapiro right in his reflective number 9. Shapiro tugged on Wang's jersey-blazer, indicating he had the ball. Wang froze in place and began aggressively pacing the incoming defenders.

Number nine had to get rid of the ball in haste as the secondary was closing in quicker than expected.

Then, out of the corner of his eye, Shapiro saw that 2WR Othello Dior would be open in now less than half a second.

Shapiro reached back and slung the ball to where he knew Dior would be in 3... 2... 1...

Caught.

TOUCHDOWN!

King Clancy churlishly waved his two fingers like a pregnant woman trying to catch a cab.

Fitzpatrick and Shapiro switched places, Regina

Alstott lined up behind Shapiro, and Keyshawn Mingo lined up right next to Fitzpatrick.

The snap.

Regina ran up and faked taking the ball into her midsection, plowing full speed into the waiting nose tackles with gusto.

Mingo sprang up from his fade route and Shapiro made the connection while being drug down.

40-39, Estes Park

58 seconds remain.

The crowd angrily took their disbelief into the one-minute warning.

The following content has been brought to you by:

Got at least

Members in your family?

Pay

Low Price.

For Dinner.

The Slick Saxon

The Jeminye twins brought their offense onto their field and lined up against the defense. The Meter-Wheel had not maintained its initial kindness towards the visiting Estes Park team today, putting them square on their own 10-meter line. Both sides were in a standard formation, raising the suspicion of both coaches.

As Cassandra read the defense and called out cadences, Coach Clancy gave a hand signal to 1SS Marcellus Reid, the defensive captain.

"Tahoe! Tahoe! Tahoe!" Reid, from his free-floating position behind the d-line, called out while smacking his helmet and making eye contact with several key defensemen.

While the last bits of the word 'Tahoe' were emitting from Reid's mouth, Cassandra snapped the ball.

2DE Declan Ngata swam around the double-team pushing him back and sprinted through open field directly towards the blonde goddess. Cassandra looked for her safety valve, but the play was blown up, thanks to Reid's last-second defensive audible.

Cassandra tucked the ball and took off, only to be sprung upon by OLB Mukesh "The Monsoon" Singh. The blow hit her just above her navel, causing an accidental Dirty Dancing lift. She managed to isolate and maintain possession of the ball as she came crashing to the ground.

When she could once more feel, she felt several blades of sod tickling the back of her neck. She opened her eyes and let them regain their focus.

The moon was full and enormous.

A thunderhead was rolling in and the wind was just starting to pick up.

Slowly the din of the crowd returned, like a stereo coming on for the first time. Her mouth guard lost its suction and detached slightly, causing her to reflexively catch it with her bottom jaw.

She could still feel the ball in her left hand; the nodules that arose on the surface of the ball had served their purpose as grip. She slowly rotated her head to the left to verify her possession, and noticed the end zone paint.

A safety.

41-40, Los Angeles, CE

32 seconds remaining.

The meter-wheel next landed on the 45-meter line on the LA side. Fitzpatrick confidently strode out, a run-only offensive package following him.

On the other side, Coach Iggy Chisholm sent out his patented Ultra-Heavy-D set: almost all nose tackles and ends, lined up tight in a grits-blitz look.

Coach Clancy called in a formation he had lifted from the Assam Creeping Death, the infamous Sikkimese Rhino.

Fitzpatrick lined up in the deep gun with two fullbacks split at two steps ahead of him. Instead of two tight ends, two nose tackles squatted in the ready position on the flanks. In the backfield, Kingdom Foxx scouted for potential holes.

The snap.

Fitzpatrick faked the handoff and began scrambling, one eye on the clock, the other on the lightning-fast monsters coming to devour him.

The scrambling persisted until he found himself surrounded by defenders. Seeing there were less than 15 seconds left on the clock, Fitzpatrick flung the ball at the only flash of pressed-suit-jersey he could make out in the sea of pixelated green and white Estes Park away jerseys.

LA Nose-tackle-turned-offensive-tackle Julek Miklaszewski caught the ball with his fingertips and, carrying three defenders on his back, duck-walked until time ran out.

Final score: 41-40, LA victory.

4

A TYPICAL SHIFT AT
A LEROY'S NARCOFLORIA

"So I was looking for something with an inviting scent and a bit of a kick."

"OK, over here we have an appetizing arrangement of Amphetdrangea nestled in a crown of night-blooming Jasmine." Niko led the symphony director over to an ornate display in the Stimulant Section.

"Oh, my goodness… that is IT!" The plentiful, wealthy, onyx-skinned socialite clapped with acceptance. She ran her delicate hands over the squid moss that bolstered the Jasmine crown. The soft shehnai and linear jazz drums misting down from the ceiling speakers caused a swell of emotion.

"I'll take it. Right now. I'll also need it replaced every fourteen days for the season."

"Absolutely."

"And can you coordinate the petal colors with the hex codes I send over?"

"Of course."

"I'd like to add a hemodilating micro rose bush to the crown."

"No problem."

"One more thing," her voice shifted.

"Anything, Madame."

She leaned in, uncomfortably close.

"Swann's Dodder; can you get it for me?"

"I-"

"Yes, or no. I need it for a party this weekend," she grabbed his forearm and relaxed her face. "I'm only asking you because we've worked together for some time now."

That was true. Ever since he abandoned his quasi-legal, secure-contract-courier venture, he had worked in the LeRoy's Narcofloria #749. On Niko's second day, Clara Gagné-Le Roux floated in and simply began talking. His boss, Bhadraksh Lipnicki, sporting the nauseating combo of a baldhead and a large beard, aggressively flexed the muscles around his transfixing violet eyes at Niko. At once, Niko leapt to attention from his mooring at the Scintillating Scents enclosure.

His unbreakable attention and admiration for her social and artistic contributions made him the perfect sales associate for her.

Sometimes she came in daily. Once, she didn't show her face for six weeks. Despite her irregular schedule, her behavior upon entering the inviting and pleasing atmosphere of LeRoy's #749 never wavered.

Niko had thus far been able to deliver on every single request from Mrs. Gagne-Le Roux. This new request not only came as a shock adjustment to the image he maintained of her in his mind, but it also gave him the slightest rush of endorphins.

When she first came in three years ago, he, like all who encounter her, was, of course, taken by her beauty; but her sharp mind and insightful wit made him putty in her hands.

"I- I, uh, yes. I can g-get you some of that. Plant." His lip shook. *What am I saying? I could be arrested!*

"Excellent…" she knew she had him from the instant she walked in. "So, how, exactly?" She fluttered her cantilevered eyelashes.

"Oh, uh," his mind raced as he tried to cook up an adult-sounding sequence of events. "I need to talk to my *guy* first," he cleared his throat. *Yeah, that sounded like Supplier talk.*

"Oh, your *guy* huh? OK, here, call me from this when you're ready to make a clean exchange, no talking," she raised her finger while handing him a shabby-looking mobile phone. "Mine is the only number in there. Destroy it after you call me, thanks!"

The spindly woman flashed a stunning smile, turned, and ushered her elegance out of the luxurious gated portion of the store. Niko breathed a sigh of relief and began filling out the customary forms for her over-the-table delivery. By now he was used to her abrupt behavior; after all, billionaires don't stay that way sitting still.

After her order was in place, Niko made a sweep of the entire sales floor. He strode from the posh gold and white Stimulants Section through the forest-themed Hallucinogenic Hollow that was drenched in a verdant green motif and fiber optic lighting. He next made a pass through the large, undersea-themed, sunken Den of Depressants.

The customers in the Stimulants Section were occupied.

Those milling about in the burgeoning tree confluence that was Hallucinogenic Hollow were preparing to watch a very old film synced to a vinyl record with a rainbow blasting prism on the cover.

In the softly lit Den of Depressants, his sweating loaf of a manager was engaged with another High-Profile customer.

Even the new-product kiosks and roving sample carts were all engaged and cared for.

This was his chance.

He ambled over to the centralized cash register system and prepared himself mentally to engage his least favorite coworker.

"Hey, Byron, you uh, you got a sec?" He leaned in and tried to sound genuinely interested in the repugnant fellow.

"...'sup Niko, yeah, I got some time," the tall and pale transplant from Vast Vegas wobbled over. His weathered skin and faded black jeans clashed against the comforting and splendid green and gold candy striped motif of the overall store.

Niko looked around and began rubbing his left hand over his mouth.

"Could you get me, uh, some, Sverfer

Derdder?"

"Some *what?*"

"Some Swann's Dodder?" He said it clearer.

"Oh, *The Creep*? Yeah, I have that… you take that?" Byron seemed surprised that Niko would want such a lurid parasite.

"Psh, yeah… my girl loves it," *What am I saying!?*

"Your girl, huh?"

"Yup," Niko pursed his lips and refused to break eye contact.

"OK, ok. Meet me in the employee greenhouse in ten."

"*Here?* You keep it *here?*" Niko was incredulous.

"*You've* never seen it, right?" The skeleton smiled.

He had a point.

Niko swallowed hard and nodded.

The light flooding in from the glass storefront made everything shimmer.

🏆

Ten minutes later, Niko was on his break and walking into the employee greenhouse. He walked passed another employee, Dalbir with the eye patch, and continued down the corridor Byron Crofts indicated.

"Psst,"

The noise sprang upon Niko like an errant steam burst.

Nearby, in an alcove Niko had never noticed

before, was Byron.

"Check this out," Byron lightly rubbed a seemingly random brick in the wall.

A click.

The touched brick slid away and a nanofarm slid out on a cantilevered platform no larger than a shoebox.

"No way," Niko looked on in awe.

Byron smirked and attached a powerful set of magnifying spectacles to his face.

"How much did you need?"

"Oh, just enough for a weekend," Niko was mad he didn't ask for a quantity from the symphony director.

"A weekend, eh? Let's see, two people, vigorous physical activity planned…"

Niko cleared his throat.

"How about four bunches? That's… sixteen grams total."

"Let's double that," Niko did not want to short his favorite customer.

"…All righty, the customer's always right, huh?"

Niko's blood ran cold.

"Hehe," his voice cracked. "Yeah, that is the idiom, isn't it?"

"Sure is, buddy." Byron turned his focus to an impossibly small pair of tweezers and plucked until he had amassed a bushel no bigger than a thimble. Clearly the man was highly adept at this method of harvest. Before the intricate nanofarm was slid back into it's housing, Niko noticed that the microscopic farm hands all wore luchador masks.

"Say, I'm a bit of a home-horticulturalist and I think I may want one of those nanofarms…" Niko baited while not trying to sound like an informant or competition.

"…You think that's cool, eh?" Byron stopped the packing process and lowered the magnifying goggles. For a time he studied Niko in silence. "All right, you're not a *Slaver*. I can tell. After three years, something would've slipped, but I can see you're cool… even if you are a little *rhomboid*…"

Niko chuckled at the subtle jibe, trying to ease his apprehension.

"Ok, well," Byron donned the goggles once more and finished up the package for Niko. "Gimme your thumb,"

Niko did as told.

Byron brought up a box no larger than a thumbprint and no deeper than a kumquat. He first placed the tiny bundle of Amplified Narcofloria contraband inside, then he took Niko's thumb and pressed it to what would be considered the top of the small container.

"There. Now only you can open it and once you do, it will self-enlarge. It's a custom carrier of my personal design and-"

"Only I can open it?" Niko cut in.

"…Yeah, nice and secure. That way if a Slaver or a Law Officer stops you, it becomes a trinket; something for a kid you know, or whatever. You can put it on your key ring. The point is they can't open it."

"OK, that makes sense." *I'm screwed.*

"All righty-dighty then. That'll be $2000GD, my friend."

What!

"Sure, sure, cool, cool, cool, n-no problem, sure." Niko slowly withdrew his wallet and lifted out his charge card.

Randy received the plastic and tapped it to his device.

And just like that, Niko was in debt.

$2000GD...

Randy removed the goggles and restored them to their storage space. He next once more lightly massaged the brick, this time causing the nanofarm to retract.

"Now about your earlier question, as to where one may find one of these miniature ventures..." their business concluded, Byron stood and began leading the way out. Niko once more marveled at how well Byron was able to hide such a thing in plain sight.

"...I'm only going to say this once. Go to the Mexican Embassy, tell them you're making a delivery, bring one of our bags. Tell them you're there to see *Mr. Peña.* Once in his office, ask about 'agricultural enterprising on a molecular level.' Those words, in that order. Slide him $100GD and leave. When you are off the premises, someone will find you and deliver your nano. This will only work because I'm vouching for you, so don't screw it up," Byron stopped and poked Niko in the chest with a cold, hard, finger. "Wait until tonight, then go."

Niko nodded and mechanically ambled back onto the sales floor, now panting and eager to end his shift.

He plodded up the exquisite green sparkling spiral stairs to the café and spa level. The acorn, as he decided to call the biometrically locked package, rattled in his pocket.

He grabbed a tray and got in line.

Ok, I'll call her when I'm off. Then I'll just tell her that only I can open it, and she'll understand...

He shuffled along and grabbed a French onion soup.

I'll go to her house, scan my thumb, she'll get her Dodder...

The person behind him prodded Niko to continue down the line. He hurriedly grabbed a piece of naan, a small palak paneer and several malai kofta.

He paid and sat down facing the portion of the store that featured several restorative Pods. The black mussels were clustered in groups; different sets of pods providing different sets of relief. He fixated on the Euphoric Group of sleek obsidian devices and briefly studied a very attractive Chinese woman settling into hers. Olga, a stout and bright-eyed Bavarian, was helping the Chinese patron with whatever she needed. Olga was attentive and arguably the best technician in her department. Her hands were pudgy but inviting. Niko had never had a session in a pod where her pleasantness didn't add to the overall experience. Surely the woman Olga was now attending to would leave a good review, really only giving their mutual superiors even more reasons to raise her pay.

The Chinese woman had green eyes and golden hair. Her skin was creamy like milk tea. The robe she wore stopped above her knee and was red silk with floral designs.

Olga held out a tray of pen-sized vaporizers. The woman chose a thin silver model; a unit contained within itself, needing no cartridge.

Olga smiled and gracefully glided over to the Pod's controls.

The woman began inhaling and eventually let out a tremendous cloud of relief. A smile came over her eyes as she lay into the angled enclosure.

Once she was clear, Olga initiated the sequence.

The lid closed.

A green hue began to seep out from inside the Pod.

Having used that particular Pod himself several times, Niko knew what the woman was experiencing. He could really use several *years* in one of those right about now.

The acorn in his pocket was rubbing into his thigh.

Is it getting hot?

Of course it wasn't.

What would happen if I were to open it prior to giving it to her?

He chose to not find out.

His meal finished, Niko felt he could not justify

hanging around to watch the beautiful woman's session come to an end.

He stacked the remnants of his now ransacked foodstuffs onto the tray and bussed it near the exit.

90 more minutes…

As he trotted down the spiral stairs, the acorn poked him.

Ouch…

Before he could really process the poke in and of itself, his purple-eyed overseer met him at the bottom of the stairs.

"Ito!" The sallow and pasty man always called Niko only by his middle name. Despite being as white as a sheet, the man's thick Delhi accent betrayed him.

"Yes, sir," Niko knew it was going to be about the Death.

"Your team lose again!" His nostrils, wide and offensive, produced more audible noise than his vocal chords.

"I know, I know, it's about the love of the *game* though, right?" Niko always had a hackneyed, rehearsed, comeback for whatever Bhadraksh had to say. Usually his barbs stopped after a few canned answers, but today he just kept following Niko around.

"Hey, Ito!"

"Yes, sir?"

"The Death will never win! Eh? Clancy and The Firm! Eh?" The man broke into a guttural laugh, simultaneously slapping Niko on the back.

"Yeah, I know, my team sucks…"

"Hey Ito! You are the one saying it!"

"Ha ha, yeah…" Niko's eyes darted around, desperately looking for a patron that may need help.

There were none.

"Hey Ito! Who's your team going to lose to next? Eh?" Bhadraksh had now begun to lightly elbow Niko in the ribs.

"I think we play Miami next," Niko responded through a sigh.

"Oh, the Commie Robots? LOSE! Hahaha…"

Niko pursed his lips and slowly nodded, merely trying to keep the peace.

Just then, another local wealthy client, the BrewMaster's wife, flowed into the lobby.

"Ito! She is mine!" Bhadraksh gave Niko a non-shove and quickly squirted away to receive the cash machine.

"Hello, hello, Madame, please, I, Bhadraksh, am at your *personal* service…" His sudden eloquence always irked Niko.

"The customer is always right…" Niko thought he heard this as the two individuals walked by.

For a few minutes, he replayed their passing in his mind, trying to discern who could've said it, if it was even said at all. The voice was smooth, but not a woman's. After that breathy exchange about his favorite team, he reasoned it had to be Bhadraksh. *Was it the idiom, or the code?*

Niko had never seen Bhadraksh anywhere near the Store, but then again, Niko rarely saw the same crew more than twice. The thought of his manager, this pig of a human, Shopping made his head spin. *How could I have not noticed him?* He reasoned that Bhadraksh's purple eyes, or his trademark hideous baldhead-full-beard combo, reminding him of a ball of used toilet paper, would've caught his attention somewhere along the lines.

When he realized he was gawking at the man he merely tolerated for the sake of employment, he broke off and dismissed the entire concept of Bhadraksh Shopping. Frankly he felt the man deserved no more of his precious brainspace. After all, tonight, Niko had to make a very important stop.

Niko was off at 1915pm.

The skeleton from Stratford-on-Avon known as Byron Crofts gave a devious smile and nod when Niko passed by him on his way out.

When Niko was far enough away from the sprawling emporium, he pulled out the dinged up phone Mrs. Gagne-Le Roux had given him. She was right. There was only one number and no means to dial another.

Niko pressed Call.

The line rang seven times.

"Hello, Niko."

"Hello, Madame."

"Come to Pattabong and ring the bell underneath the golden pineapple," the line went dead.

Everyone in Darjeeling knew where the golden pineapple was. The statuette had been the final item on a famous and storied scavenger hunt. Local Yogi Anjan Malik had found it in a necropolis and was carried into the city on the shoulders of his supporters for his discovery.

Niko skipped the trip to his apartment and instead hired a bike from a city bike-share kiosk.

He clicked and pedaled across town, through the late rush hour, across the great Vinod Boulevard, and around the pillars of the Sri Gupta Elevated Park and Gardens.

When he arrived in Pattabong, the sun had just set. A red and orange wash had appeared and consumed the locale. The golden pineapple rested on a perch in front of a smoldering blues venue. Tonight, a bayou legend, Hercule Breadsalt and The Shakers were headlining a show opened by Blame It On Adolf. The dueling genres of Adolf's technical EDM Death Metal juxtaposed with Breadsalt's virile Southern Sludge Blues made Niko's mouth water. For a brief second he contemplated buying a ticket and leaving the acorn in a 'safe' place for Mrs. Gagne-Le Roux to find, but common sense got the better of him.

He crept up to the lone golden fruit and jostled it. The cluster tipped over and exposed a red button.

Niko depressed it.

Not two-minutes later did a gray-skinned little person emerge from a previously unnoticed set of doors. He tugged on Niko's sleeve to get his attention. Niko looked down into the mustachioed man's triangular face.

"Dis whey," he said while immediately heading off in the direction indicated.

Niko was led down an alley that featured a small creek on the left-hand side. On the right were a collection of VHS dens. Niko looked into every other den and smirked at the old men and women corralled in beanbag chairs and huddled around LCD TVs playing last century's forgotten art pieces.

The smell of cinnamon and cardamom rolled in like a fog.

"Now 'ere come de tricky part..." the little gray man said without looking back.

Niko was pulled through a winding maze of narrow alleys and tight pockets of Darjeeling he had never seen before.

More random creeks.

A few private, fenced off, gardens.

A personal zoo.

After fifteen minutes of continuous twists and turns, the little gray man pointed to a set of stairs that arose from a street Niko had never seen before and disappeared up into a bamboo tunnel.

"She is up der," the man said before causally walking off and into an Adults Only club nearby.

"Uh, thanks," Niko responded. He slid the acorn out of his pants pocket and clutched in his right hand. He looked around and observed the class of people well suited to the affluence of the area. No one cared to notice him, so he began his climb into the darkness.

The steps went on and on.

Eventually the bamboo shuddered and a section peeled away at random.

"Hello, Niko."

"Hello, Madame."

Niko cut right and stepped into the break in foliage. After he was in, the bamboo restored itself. He turned around after watching the plants move and took in the symphony director's play area. All around they were surrounded by dense bamboo. The spot was tiered into three levels: the topmost had three jacuzzi's and a wet bar, the middle level had sunken seating areas and speakers camouflaged as rocks, and the lowest level was a thriving Japanese-inspired narcotic garden. Mrs. Gagne-Le Roux gave Niko a small kiss on each cheek, which was her custom. She wore a tiger striped bikini and a blinding white wig. Her breasts were obsidian watermelons held back by napkins at their breaking point. Her deep black skin was accented by the gems she had stuck to her self in an intricate arrangement around her navel, up her arms, and down her legs.

"Well, Niko, *were we able to adopt a Dodder?*" she asked with a sly grin. Several others nearby, half dressed and physically perfect, gave vapid chuckles of approval.

Niko let out a fractured laugh soaked in nervousness and opened his sweaty palm.

"What is that?" She had no idea what Niko was holding out to her.

"It's uh, it's…" Niko fumbled with the orange

bobble. He righted it, and himself, and scanned his thumb in the depression that was designed just for that purpose.

The acorn leapt from his hand.

It landed on the ground directly in front of the symphony director.

In an instant, six black ceramic pots full of the illegal plants swelled into existence.

"Oh my!" Mrs. Gagne-Le Roux popped her eyes and dropped her drink. "Did I order too much? How did this set you back?"

"Uh, well, it cost $2000GD up front, and then the transport-"

"Ooh, that's cheap! Here, keep the change," Clara used her thumb to authorize a transfer of $50,000GD directly into Niko's deficient account. He was stunned at the carefree attitude she displayed. 'Keep the change' she told him. He wouldn't make the change in another seven months of daily overtime.

The crop burgeoned forth from its horticultural lodging. The other half-dressed people all directed agog expressions towards their next meal.

"Who's first?" Clara called without taking her eyes from the quivering mass of black market foliage.

Pierre Mountbatten Bhowmick, a slim and empty-headed Bengali slithered up to the mass wearing a thonged speedo. He extended his left arm, his right hand was occupied with a glass of spearmint absinthe, and waited for the plant to take action. Within seconds, the vine produced a tendril to match Pierre's. The parasitic pseudopodia grafted itself onto

121

Pierre's arm. Instantly, tiny little buds began to bloom all over Pierre's body. The others oohed and awwed at the floral Indian from Puducherry.

Clara Gagne-Le Roux scooped a handful of the miniscule blossoms and shoved them into her mouth. They were washed down with whatever green alcohol was in her glass and several drags on her seventeen-inch cigarette holder. The smoking stump contained a powerful opium and hashish mélange.

After Clara, the other dozen or so half-naked humans each took a handful and began chewing.

"Can I, can I go?" Niko spoke up after fifteen minutes of gorging and groping.

Clara pulled herself from another privileged Indian and planted her pillowy lips directly onto Niko's.

"Leaving so soon? Oh well, THANK YOU darling, you may leave the way you came in..." she turned and walked away. Niko noticed she was longer wearing anything below her navel. With a flick of her wrist, the bamboo peeled away again and revealed once more the dark and seemingly endless tunnel.

Niko walked over to his exit. He stood in the opening and watched for another few minutes. The revelers all started sprouting pea-sized flowers and consuming each other. Some took to the hot tubs. Others planted themselves in front of the LED screens and enjoyed whatever played. A few secured themselves in the garden and ingested even more psychoactive plant material. Clara was a goddess in her personal hot tub. A disco ball rose from the center of a rose bush. Pulsing beats from Clara's favorite DJ duo, Old Man Fosdick, flooded the area from hidden speakers. Niko wanted to stay and watch but once more, common sense prevailed. He turned and began his journey home.

"Farewell, gorgeous Niko! See you at the emporium!" Clara called out from a floral mass of flesh and hot water.

The bamboo sealed itself shut following his exit.

At the bottom of the steps, Niko found his way out via a trail of fireflies, he was met by the gray little man.

"Mmm, dis vhey," he said. The small fellow now wore a bright blue sari and a yellow hardhat. Niko followed him back through the maze, along the creek, and passed the never-empty VHS dens.

As soon as he was back in an area he was familiar with, the gray man vanished. Niko rented another bike and pedaled home in the darkness.

The following content has been brought to you by:

If it's 3ʳᵈ and long
and you're Feelin' Weak,

THEN IT'S...

POWER CHOWDER™

THAT YOU SEEK!

CRACK A CAN AND SUCK IT DOWN
THEN GET BACK OUT THERE
& SACK THAT CLOWN!

The combined raw power of 17 unique species of clam <u>CAN'T</u> be wrong!

It's what you seek!®

5

MEET THE QUARTERBACK

Saxby Nerva Lawless kneaded his right ankle with his paw-like hands. The mornings after a game, especially after a loss, were never easy. He sat on the edge of his bed, the clock reading 0730am, and shrugged the pain from his shoulders several times. As he stood, his neck and back popped and cracked, the stolid bubbles releasing their nitrogen into his blood stream.

"Floors, please."

The heated bamboo flooring kicked on.

Behind him, his wives lay sleeping still, tangled in the cotton sheets and blankets Saxby looked forward to after every game, no matter where it was and what happened.

From his redbrick penthouse bedroom, Saxby shuffled to his Greenhouse and groped for one of his precious tramadol-daffodils. He plucked several stalks and mechanically began chewing the buds. Within the span of several seconds, the reality he was accustomed to returned. He next stopped at one of the many wall-mounted Phaelenopsis-Aquae and parked his mouth directly underneath its column. The flower sprang into action and began pouring its Amplified distillate into the storied 1QB's throat.

After several minutes of deep and satisfying gulps, Saxby noticed his blonde wife from Dorset had gotten up and was preparing his breakfast.

"Thank you, Charlotte, I love you," he called as he ambled over to his sitting area.

Saxby stepped down into a sunken room lined with a tremendous wrap-around couch. His spot was at the dead center of the room, made complete with a small table at his knees for food and whatnot. He turned on his Enveloping Holovision, the latest in H.V. tech, and told the channel to change from the UN 24-hour News Service over to the British Sports Vein.

Several minutes later, Charlotte walked in, wearing only a ribbed A-shirt and some tiny shorts that let her rear peek out, and set down his customary breakfast: a scoop of beans, three fried eggs, seven rashers of bacon, three large flek sausages, a grilled mackerel filet, a scoop of roasted spinach, a scoop of roasted Brussels sprouts, several pieces of garlic infused naan bread, a tall glass of blackberry juice, a bottle of sparkling water, and a large mug of Erythroxl-Chai tea.

Saxby gave his wife a kiss and a smack on the butt as the broadcast turned its attention to The League.

"What a comeback last night!" The animated and bombastic Nigel Foster had chosen to lead with a recap of the exciting match the night before.

"Yeah Nige," former Yeoman Warder Dickey Dover interjected. "I for one did not see Clancy and that Firm of his coming back like *that*. I'm sure Mukesh Singh has stashed away that game ball as a nice souvenir."

"Right you are, Dickey. Highlight time…"

Saxby sighed and continued gorging on his morning feast. His ire with their decision to cover the previous night's game first, featuring the team his former coach had abandoned him for, definitely arose from hurt pride.

Up until an embarrassing performance in the Night of the High Scores last season, Saxby was considered the Platinum standard for Elite, Hall-of-Fame bound 1QB's. The Amplified Gentry had virtually no need for a defense as Saxby scored whenever he set foot on the field. His mind was a tireless dynamo, producing schemes to outwit opposing defenses on-the-fly based on what he saw at the line. His cadence was legendary, and his post-game analysis emboldened more players to become coaches after retiring from playing.

Saxby himself was approaching his 25th season in The League. Only three others were longer tenured: the human-to-computer coach of Münich, the Meinhardt Vogt, Paris 1QB Amplified Napoleon Bonaparte, and The King himself, Clancy Chesterfield. Granted, the world of Amplified Botany had contributed greatly to the physical aspects of the game, even allowing for instant-healing in some cases.

But regardless of how many times you can be easily put back together, each week every player basically endured several dozen auto-accidents on the field of play.

Saxby's ankle bothered him again so he called out for another tramadol-daffodil. His second wife, Maly from Phnom Penh, appeared in a loose ikat kimono with his request.

At last, after rich in-depth coverage of the night's previous match, the hosts guided the shows attention to the local team, The London Amplified Gentry.

"…And how about them 'Gents, eh?" Dickey Dover led off with the un-official tagline for the team.

"More like 'how could they keep starting him?'" Nigel didn't waste any time throwing Saxby under the bus. "I mean, it's the first game of the season, you're at home, every body's excited, and you lose, to the Yanks, who still cling to the ideas born from the Great Land Giveaway of 1776. Frankly, I don't think I can stomach much more of this, not after last year Dickey…"

"Bollocks!" Saxby hollered at the HV.

"Seriously. We certainly have beaten that dead horse quite a bit over the past several months, but Nige, is that horse truly *dead*?"

"Dickey, I watched last year's championship game several times in the off-season, most likely because I *hate* myself, and I just couldn't piece it together. A season like that, phenomenal, record-breaking even, and then to arrive at the Big Dance and… and… just *suck*, so bad."

"That's a bit harsh, eh Nige?"

"No, Dickey, I don't think so. As Londoners, we are *entitled* to excellence, and yes! Sterling Carberry, Saxby Lawless and the rest have, up until last season, delivered on such expectation. But what we saw take place…" the gray-looking man vigorously shook his head. "*London deserves better*, and last night only further proved *that* point…"

Saxby waved the HV to another channel and resumed gorging.

His wives knew to let him finish eating before trying to comfort him.

He took a large swig of his sparkling water and let out a raucous belch.

"Ladies, sweethearts, the loves of my life…"

"Yes,"

"Uh huh,"

"I think this season is my last ride."

The women could only maintain a cautiously hopeful silence.

This topic had come up a few times in the past. Once after a particularly scathing article in the Times, and again after a rather Pyrrhic victory over Miami two years prior.

Both times, though, Saxby responded to those calling for his retirement with two MVP trophies, two Council Cups, and two new passing records.

This idea coming forth from himself, on its own, was unspoiled land for him and his family.

"The kids will be happy," Charlotte said.

Saxby's head shot up and he regarded her with an intensity that almost immediately faded.

"They'll be thrilled," he said resignedly. But within that resignation was just enough of a smile for his lover to notice.

He was really going to do it.

Maly scooted closer to him and caressed his face with the back of her hand. Both women immediately knew how their husband would behave going forward in the season, and thus exchanged looks of mutual understanding.

"As far as I'm concerned, Sunday never happened," Saxby gruffly let out as Maly's caressing turned into a topless shoulder massage.

Charlotte brought up the schedule on her device and noted that they would be traveling to Peru to face the Obsidian Pumas of the Restored Incan Empire in a few days. This would be a tough match, especially after the loss, the critique, and the decision to retire at the end of the season.

Saxby finished his breakfast, made love to his wives, said goodbye to his plethora of children, and then departed for the team's facility in Deptford.

Upon arrival, all in attendance knew something was different about him. There was a spring in his step. He said hello to everyone present.

After warm-ups, he gathered the team together and explained his decision. Some cried, some applauded, and a few vets who still hadn't yet drank from the Cup grumbled.

When practice concluded, Saxby took his time

walking back to the tube station. On the way, he wordlessly passed one of the many ubiquitous Power Chowder HyperAds that bore his likeness. A deep breath cleared the subtle anxiety that came with the memories of shooting those ads, and having to drink all that Amplified Clam Chowder. "It's what you seek!" Saxby had said straight into the camera after a thick and chunky gulp of creamy white mollusk-born electrolytes. The crisp Lewisham air reminded him of a game played in his rookie year.

Down by 28 in the third, the old London 1QB Neville Nettles went down with a compound femur fracture. He had wiggled free from a broken play and was making headway down the sidelines when he was tackled into an old camera truck. The snapping sound made more than a few people nauseous.

Then-coach Clancy Chesterfield told Saxby to put his helmet on and execute the plays "exactly as called." Saxby tried this for one series, but lost faith in Clancy's ability to read the defense when the blitzes kept getting worse with each play.

On the next series, Saxby did what he was trained to do: he read the defense, diagnosed their intent, and communicated the distillation to the offense.

The play resulted in a touchdown, much to Clancy's ire.

To this day, Saxby Lawless still could not determine why Clancy was so mad about the score.

Sure, the rookie disobeyed a direct order and got lucky, but a W is a W, right? He would muse to himself.

When Clancy was fired four seasons later, Saxby chose to confront The King about the issue.

"Coach?"

"Yeah, Lawless?" The bald pink man answered with a hint of agitation in his voice.

"Look, I have no problem with you, let's just get that straight,"

Clancy remained silent, preoccupied with emptying his office.

"...But I just have to know why you were so upset after my first time at the controls?"

Clancy stopped what he was doing and stood still with his back to Saxby.

After a time, the man spoke.

"Son, there are things at work here in this world you couldn't even begin to comprehend," he started, but then stopped, regarding the towering Lawless with his left hand. "Let's just leave it at this: you disobeyed your coach."

"That's not enough and you know it-"

"Quit while you're ahead son, you'll regret it if you keep pushing me."

"I'll regret it?"

Swiftly turning around and catching Saxby off

guard, Clancy reached up and stuck his right index finger square into Saxby's chest.

"*Do not test me, boy,*" Clancy said through his teeth without blinking.

All Saxby could do was put up his hands in a show of innocence and leave in a stunned silence.

The smell of the tube station wiped out the thought train he had been riding up to that point.

That night, as he lay in bed with Charlotte and Maly, he made a promise to himself. Saxby swore to make this the most outlandish and stat-destroying season he had every played. If Saxby Nerva Lawless was going out, he was going out with a *bang*.

Saxby carefully slid out of bed, not disturbing his goddesses, and tip toed to the sprawling greenhouse. He walked down a corridor full of creeping vines and arrived at the inner sanctum of a glass construct.

In here was a specimen he acquired from an outgoing legend of the game, Aurelius Swann. This plant had been spliced with a hematopoietic stem cell, allowing for it to produce human leukocytes. The only problem was the confluence of Cuscuta and Pilostyle DNA. As it stood, the Swann's Dodder lived parasitically on a large cannabis stalk Saxby had arranged for it. Swann explained that the plant could not survive without a host, and that the host needed to be changed regularly, as it would eventually run out of nutrients.

Saxby chose a cannabis stalk as its perpetual dormant-state-host due to the sedative and euphoric effect the Swann's Dodder would receive.

As Saxby looked over the impressive growth, he recalled a warning Aurelius had given him: "Be careful with your exposure time. Remember, it *needs* a host to survive, and if it's on you for too long, you will meld…"

"Meld…" Saxby said out loud as he stroked the pulsating tendrils. He thought briefly about his family, but then shooed away any thoughts of concern for them.

Saxby reached up and tore several tendrils and buds from their station and consumed them, whole. The stalks were tough and fibrous, but the buds popped like syrup filled candies, lubricating the tendrils as he swallowed. Aurelius Swann had told him to eat no more than two handfuls at a time. Saxby drove right passed that thought and consumed until he was *full*.

His rite finished, Saxby returned his bed. As he fell into a deep sleep, Maly slyly woke Charlotte and stole her away to review the footage from the camera that Saxby didn't know about.

6

Niko got lost in the items he had been scanning. Each blip that emitted from the register indicating a purchase seemed to change key with every third item.

Was that one an F#? He thought.

The Customer he was currently engaged with was an Executive VP. She was farm-girl pale with sharp features and flawless, satin skin. Her San Francisco accent made her stand out amongst the cockney rank and file of this particular Store, which happened to be in London. Niko's normal Store in Darjeeling was fine, but this branch needed a Clerk III for a few weeks while a suitable replacement was sourced.

In between items, Niko would steal a glance at the statuesque woman in front of him. Her neck looked like a perfect fit for his lips. Her golden hair was flat; each strand looking as it if it were deliberately placed. Her top lip flared up slightly, accentuating her overbite and exposing a millimeter or two of her incisors. Her eyes were a very crisp and understated hazel with sharp green flecks strewn about the iris. Her weak chin dribbled into her neck, and her breasts, larger than grapefruits, sat a little low and hooked up, causing a void to form in her blouse. He briefly

135

imagined the two of them sitting in a green Nissan Figaro, listening to some of her favorite music, whatever that was. She would be wearing a floral print dre-

"Excuse me? Clerk?"

"Oh, uh, sorry," Niko was pulled back to reality by the woman herself.

"I'm quite eager to get to the *Bistro*, are we almost done?" Her nasally voice was like a crisp and soothing harmonium.

The way the words happily left her soft, inviting lips almost sent him on another trip.

"Oh, y-yes, I'm sorry miss," Niko quickly scanned the rest of her items and bagged them.

"How long have you been a Clerk III?" She asked, gently knitting her brow.

"Oh, uh, I was just promoted."

"But, you're not from Britannia. I can tell."

"Oh, no, I'm from Darjeeling, but King Clancy said this branch needed a hand after an incident of some kind," Niko was forcing his voice to remain steady. She was just so beautiful!

"Oh, you serve under King Clancy…" her eyes took on an awkward sultriness that only made things harder for Niko, in more ways than one.

"If you really do serve under K.C., then I know you watched the match last night," hers was a tone of seriousness.

"Of course! I mean, yes, I watched it."

"Do you think LA will do it this year? Go undefeated?"

"If Clancy has his way and arrives at the big dance with all those bonus chips, I can't see how he couldn't."

"...But what about the Creeping Death?" she bit her bottom lip and leaned closer, just to mess with him.

"W-What gave me away?"

"Believe it or not, K.C. likes die-hard fans of ho-hum teams, no offense," they both chuckled at the pun. "But I must say," the woman digressed. "The front office there is atrocious! Seventeen different 1QB's in a dozen seasons? Eight head coaches, six GM's..."

"Yeah, you gotta love the team and the town more than the owners. That's for true," Niko said with a sigh.

"What do you like about Assam and Darjeeling in particular?"

"To be honest, I partly grew up on a tea plantation, and I just got used to the way time flows throw there. Tea Garden Time is hard to shake when you've grown up with it."

"That's it, though? The time zone?"

"Well, no, not just that. But that is powerful," Niko searched his mind for reasons. "While Darjeeling does suit my circadian rhythm better, the air, the people, the energy from the Earth... there are actually a lot of things, now that I think about it."

The woman moved in a little closer and caught hold of Niko's desire. "Would I like it there?" she asked, without breaking eye contact, her verdant eyes reminded him of a translucent cup of hojicha tea.

Niko was at a loss for words and began fumbling his lips.

"Well," she continued, "I may just find out as you've just earned your first *Good Reference*." The seductive woman reached into an inner pocket of her sleek purple blazer and withdrew a green snakeskin tri-fold piece of card stock. She unfolded it fully, pulling back the two door-like flaps. She next reached into her right pocket and affixed a gold coin with a red ribbon to the rightmost panel. The emblem on the coin reflected the Store she represented, the very Store the two of them now stood in.

"Congratulations, Niko," she said as she leaned in to give him a kiss on the cheek. She held her lips there for a nanosecond longer than one normally would. As she pulled back, her scent paraded past his nose in a forceful procession. Lychee, sandalwood, bergamot... The bouquet was unforgettably complex.

"Now give me my groceries, *I have to start cooking!*" She told him sternly.

He took the tri-fold certificate and tucked it into his shirt pocket. He finished ringing her up and made sure she could handle the bulging bags he had just prepared for her.

Niko couldn't help but watch her leave, something she was keenly aware of. She let him enjoy the show guilt-free. From the side, her rear was a perfect cantilevered teardrop that maintained a jiggling bulbousness near the rear-thigh/cheek division line. Niko estimated her to have about a size 8 pants size, but with a complementary 27-30 inch waist.

Niko returned to checking out his line of Customers, all higher-ranked than he. No one else started, or was eager to maintain, a conversation, but Niko appreciated this. He took the time he had ringing up customers to kick around and analyze his experience with the Executive VP. *What was her name?!* He briefly panicked. Only the Clerks were required to wear nametags, and everyone knew the Kings off-hand. The Uppers, however, were under their own volition when choosing whether or not to share their names.

Niko then remembered the Certificate she had given him. The gold coin she used would bear her name, as it was only hers to give.

He withdrew the document from his pocket and opened it. There, on the bottom on the coin it read: Margeaux Drexler.

Right away Niko knew that what he heard the other night on the sports news broadcast was not a slip-up. The Hall-of-Famer 1QB Lamont Drexler had said a code word, live, worldwide, on holovision. *No wonder he immediately broke into a sweat,* Niko thought. *King Clancy would not be happy.*

After his shift was over, Niko decided to head to the only part of the *Bistro* that Clerks were allowed in, the Viewing Gallery.

Like an operating theatre, Clerks could look down on their superiors, Executive VP's, King's, and Viceroy's, and watch them indulge and cajole. Niko often found himself staring into the open kitchen, watching the men and women clad in white swiftly move about.

Turning his attention to the floor, Niko tried to memorize the faces he was seeing. He could make out two Kings, a dozen or so Viceroys, and too many Executive VP's to count.

One King sat at a long table. He was the only man seated there, and the women lining the sides varied in shape and race.

The other King sat alone, in a dark corner, at a small round table, wearing a tartan pattern.

Just as Niko had worked up the courage to ask a Local who the two King's were, the entire building shuttered.

The kitchen ground to a halt.

All diners put down their flatware and finished whatever was in their mouths.

Several, but not all, houselights came up and revealed a large stage near what would be considered the top of the room.

How did I miss that? He thought.

The green harlequin curtains were pulled back and King Clancy emerged to uproarious applause. Shortly thereafter, several recognizable LA Firm players followed, dragging along a man in fetters and chains with a bag over his head.

After the chants died down, Clancy spoke.

"Hello family," the customary greeting, when addressing a large group of vested Customers, trumpeted from his lips.

"Many of you may have seen the PolyMatic

Highlight Show Broadcast earlier tonight and you may have heard something a little familiar…" He baited the crowd. Boos and hisses, along with grumbling and the occasional "Drexler" could be heard.

Clancy walked over, his spurred cowboy boots certifying each step, to the man with a sack on his head. In a smooth motion, the bag was removed, and Lamont Drexler exposed.

"You've betrayed our order!"

"Scandal!"

"Fool!"

"Charlatan!"

The calls came from all over the Bistro.

King Clancy held his hands over his head and sued for peace before pronouncing his judgment.

"Lamont Van Allen Drexler, this is your *Second* strike. One more, and you'll have to endure a Loving Spoonful…" Niko, of course, had been briefed on the penalty system and was unfortunate enough to have witnessed several disciplinary events similar to this one. The Loving Spoonful though, he had not yet had the privilege to observe. The *Customer Buttcheeks Handbook* had a one-line definition:

The Loving Spoonful:
(CAN ONLY BE ADMINSITERED BY A KING+)
K presents trusty sack-o-pills. One scoop per out.

"You," King Clancy continued. "Are hereby *De*moted to Executive VP. II, and must report to *me* weekly until further notice."

The other Clerk's in the viewing gallery gasped as their blood ran cold. This demotion meant the world famous individual was back to waiting tables, forced to eat only the Staff Meal.

"I don't think he can do it..." Niko heard another behind him say.

On stage, Lamont Drexler silently cried.

King Clancy threw the bag back onto the man's head and waved goodbye to the London Store.

Another shudder for the whole building as the Rosenbridge granted passage for the King and his cadre to return to The Capitalist Empire of Los Angeles.

Why did he have to do that here? Niko wondered. Before his thought train could depart its usual station, Niko felt a pair of eyes burning into him from afar.

From the Kitchen, Niko could see Margeaux, staring straight at him. Her unwavering focus did more than any speech could have. Although not fully aware of what just took place, he could discern from Margeaux's look, the words of the other Clerks, and Clancy's behavior that something wasn't quite right.

The "please remove yourselves" light, as it had come to be called, came on in the Viewing Gallery. All the Clerks, Niko included, now had to leave as the Uppers on the Bistro floor below entered what Niko knew to be called Executive Session. It was in these Sessions that world-affecting decisions were made. Probably.

Uppers were strictly forbidden from sharing the contents of an Executive Session, under the penalty of immediate expulsion. Additionally, if you did spill some tea and share what happened in a Session, your life would be ruined. Only the King's knew the true number of Customer's worldwide, or so the rumor goes, and once you are out, entire cities and nation-states could potentially stop speaking to you entirely. In truth, one would cease to exist to all vested members, however many that was globally.

Margeaux never stopped looking at Niko the entire time the Clerks were being shuffled out. He turned and stole one last look before he was completely out of the room. She winked.

The following content has been brought to you by:

Omar Gilligan's
Discount

Electro-Domestics!

"Plug it in, and it works!"

7

OUR KING

King Clancy marched into his study, thirsty for his traditional post-game potable: a tumbler of stern Islay Malt that had the privilege of preserving a Malayan Krait. Clancy studied the bottle very closely before pouring his allotment.

The bottle was about twenty centimeters high and was made of clear glass. At the bottom were various herbs and berries: some goji's, a coca leaf or seven, a tangle of ginseng. The snake was caught by a friend of the King's at 0200am in the outskirts of Taiping, and shipped alive to his palatial home in The Armored Beverly Hills. Once arrived, Clancy sedated the snake with his own blend of papaver and lorazepam. Clancy would then artfully slip the limp snake into an empty bottle. Next, he would take a metal skewer and stimulate the venom sacs to bring forth their potion. From there, Clancy took the now prepared bottle to his cellar. He kept a tremendous barrel of his favorite smoky Islay Scotch on the backs of five small elephants he carved himself from redwood. The cask itself was engulfed in a scaled-down genetically engineered redwood forest. Clancy had grown to admire the great redwood forests just north of Japanese San Francisco, as he had been taught to call it. The genuine Bermuda grass floor made the feeling of sacredness complete. The bottle was topped off, then sealed, and finally racked until game day.

Before he would leave for a game, Clancy would retrieve one of his bottles and nestle it into a grove of miniature Giant Sequoias. The noble trees grew, espousing vitality and cause for reverence, out of his countertop and into the shape of a perch. Here, the carefully sourced and prepared bottle would patiently wait for him until he returned victorious.

Reaching into his antique tumbler hutch, Clancy carefully chose a uranium crystal glass so unique it seemed to hum in his hands. This victory was special and thus called for a special glass.

He turned from his preparation and located his favorite overstuffed leather chair. His study was positioned in the top level of the third and final spire that arose from the dark brick and ivy covered manor. The western wall was made entirely of diamond pane windows that overlooked the throbbing metropolis.

Clancy paused and decided yes, this victory also called for that which could get him arrested, *Decommissioned*, and so on. He sauntered confidently over to one of his many bookshelves and tugged on a signed copy of How To Hate by Dr. Alyona Romanova. This book had been rigged to open a hidden door directly behind the bookcase. As the door slid open, Clancy embraced the rich and enlivening smell of cured tobacco.

Despite the ban imposed almost immediately after UN Victory, Clancy decided his one permissible vice would be a combustible and perfunctory source of nicotine.

Here in the outermost room, the curing was done. Leaves that Clancy himself had harvested were prepared and then aged in accordance with a methodology learned from an old journal he had found while on vacation in The Carolinas. Before filling his pipe and rolling a cigar and three cigarettes, his post-game custom, Clancy decided to admire his small but formidable farm.

The aquaponic system he designed and built himself had trout and red-clawed crayfish as its foundation. A large u-shaped pond wrapped around the room behind the bookcase. Clancy stood and watched the fish flitter about, while the crayfish migrated almost continuously from one end of the pond to the other. Above the creatures and in verdant towers was an allotment of companion plants, all serving to propagate and maintain several heaving tobacco strains. The leaves were richly green and the LED lighting made the entire arrangement appear as if it were breathing. The increase in oxygen gave him momentary light-headedness. Clancy closed the door on his adept and proficient apparatus and selected a couple choice smoked trout filets, also curing alongside some tobacco, and placed them on a dark metal serving plate.

Next, he filled his pipe with Navy Cavendish

Virginia tobacco and packed the bowl of the long stemmed half bent Billiard pipe. Clancy set the pipe in its hand-carved lounging apparatus and sprinkled Latakia tobacco into a cigar wrap. He set that aside in a pewter holster shaped like an eagle's claw. Lastly, Clancy rolled out three thin snakes of Kashmiri hashish. He laid them side-by-side on an abalone shell and then prepared three cigarette papers. He reached into his cigarette tobacco hopper and retrieved enough for the three cigarettes before him. The Perique tobacco rained down and created a bed in which the snakes would be lain; one snake per cigarette.

Clancy first lit his pipe, tucked the remaining death sticks into his plush robe pocket, and initiated the closing process.

Clancy used to be like every other upstanding UN citizen who hated the very thought of inhaling tobacco. The cavalier smell of a heavily processed cigarette used to be enough to send him into a rage. But one day, Clancy noticed a group of Latin gang members all sucking on white sticks. Then he noticed their crosstown black rivals doing the same. Clancy mused on a notion that perhaps, although fully aware of the inherent danger of smoking, the gangbangers all *chose* to smoke regardless. This led to Clancy wondering why someone would make *that* choice, especially given their respective situations as gangbangers. From his childhood, Clancy dredged up memories of kids who fell to that way of life: no parents, or overworked "parents", emotional and psychological abuse at home and at school, pressure to make other insecure kids feel not so insecure through acting out violently, economic depression... Then Clancy thought about the recidivism among that group of humanity. No matter how times you arrest or punish them, they simply keep going in the same rut. Then one day, after mentally berating a group of young REDroiders chain smoking in an alley, it hit him:

A gangbanger is someone who hates themselves more than a human could ever love anything, yet inside they remain such scared, cowardly children, they won't address their issues and end their suffering. Instead they lash out at the world around them, subconsciously begging others to put them to death. However, when their begging goes unanswered, they choose to remove themselves from society in a retributory fashion by smoking cigarettes, driving like maniacs, playing with guns, and destroying women; including the whole world in their selfish and slow suicide.

Clancy used to hate when gangbangers would smoke. But now he took comfort in their self-deletion. Every now and then he would ruminate on how this concept of conscious removal from society is what ultimately led him to the point of usage.

Again, if anyone found out he regularly partook of this particular dried indulgence, he would be relegated to labor in the redoubtable UN C.R.E.W. (Correction. Rehabilitation. Education. Work.) program; his reputation tarnished. For whatever reason, the UN had chosen to aggressively pursue and punish to the point of example anyone who harvested tobacco for combustion and inhalation. All of this had led Clancy to conceal his apparatus in the third, hardest-to-observe spire of his proto-castle.

Clancy planted himself in his favorite chair. From his robust pipe he drew in the thick, unforgiving smoke into his lungs. The rich and velvet particulate matter tickled his alveoli, which had been recently restored via a black market pollen inhalation treatment. The smoke soon became a fog. All around him Clancy could see less and less of his sanctum. He set his pipe in its chair-side caddy and turned his attention to the roaring fire at his feet. He stared at the flames while he mechanically slipped one of his three hashish cigarettes in between what passed for his lips and clicked on the old-style plasma TV above it.

He laughed and cajoled with the commentators, as if they could *actually* hear him, while they recapped his providential comeback win over the Simulacra.

Next to his right armrest was a micro hydroponic garden of hardy chewable perennials. One such, and a personal favorite, was the Mediterranean spurge he had crossbred with some rare phenethylamines. The little buds didn't break down easily when chewed, and gave Clancy the feeling he sought: that of *chewing* tobacco, but with the bonus of not losing half of his face.

The hoots and hollers that now emitted from the large study echoed throughout the house. Clancy lived alone, and he liked it that way.

Several times in the past he had tried marriage out, but the women simply weren't rugged enough to deal with a full spread PolyMatic schedule. Or at least that's what he told himself and others who asked, ignoring the plethora of players and their families that happily traveled the world as a result of the schedule. If anything, The PolyMatic Football League was geared towards maintaining cohesive and strong family units and values.

If ever he did feel lonely, Clancy would call a local elite Geisha service that was unmatched in providing something called the "Immersive Girlfriend Experience". His large, *large*, salary and savings afforded him the luxury of having a rotating gallery of women that gleefully feigned genuine interest in his ramblings. He would always request three girls of varying shapes and sizes to come and simply live their lives in his palatial brick and garden-laden manor. He would pay their bills. He would cook for them. He would listen to their issues for as long as they would listen to his.

Most of the women eventually did come to genuinely enjoy and look forward to spending time with him. The women organized an intricate and competitive pool to see who would get to go whenever he called. They began viewing the times they spent with Clancy as micro-vacations due to how well he treated them.

Really though, Clancy cared only for one thing, and it wasn't them, or even the game.

When Clancy joined Customer Buttcheeks

several years earlier, he embraced the ideals, and the 'goal', with gusto.

His father left the family at an early age and his mother was subsequently drafted by the UN. He and his siblings were rounded up and placed into the UN KinderCarousel, a somewhat helpful, but oftentimes brutal, glorified orphanage network.

When he was Of Age, Clancy was reunited with his mother, Ambassador III Irene Chesterfield. The loving and jovial woman in his memory was now a stolid bureaucrat.

"I had to change," she would say.

"You left us like he did," Clancy would respond.

Over time, the two would communicate every now and then via handwritten letters. On one occasion though, Clancy's mother sent him a package.

It was small and rattled when he shook it. He opened it in his room at the University he was attending in Beijing and discovered a note and a flash memory card.

DO NOT SHARE
-LOVE MOM

Clancy picked up an old laptop and disabled the NIC and other antennas. He slid the card in and learned one of the numerous hidden truths about the UN and their particular method of governance, specifically the beginnings of a plan to relocate the mobile capital city of New Thebes off-world.

Ever since his mother was drafted into service, despite her being a low-income highly educated single-mother, Clancy never could allow himself to fully trust the UN.

Then one day, not too long after his revelation, Clancy stumbled upon a green door in the middle of a wall. He looked around at the throng of people going through their daily lives. It was as if no one else could see the door. It was near the 中秋節 (Forbidden City) and the streets were packed. How anyone could miss or ignore this iridescent viridian entry way was baffling.

Clancy cautiously approached and as he reached for the handle, a hand shot out and speedily pulled him in.

After he was thoroughly indoctrinated, he knew *this* was where he belonged in the world.

He took his time at each rank, really savoring the flavor of servitude. His aisles were the neatest, his checkout lines went the quickest, his food was enlivening, and as a King he was unmatched in generosity and discipline.

Clancy poured so much of himself into Customer Buttcheeks that none was left for anyone else. It simply just wouldn't be fair.

Clancy's hoots, outbursts, and reactions to the game highlights also traveled down his own personal Hall of Fame. This long corridor that featured a glass ceiling maintained several pedestals that proudly displayed his achievements over the years: seven

Council Cups, four Coach-of-the-Year awards, two Gentleman Callers, a plethora of signed jersey's, thick pieces of sod from his first win and every Cup win thereafter...

King Clancy Chesterfield was certainly proud of the life he had built for himself after escaping the KinderCarousel. Even though some of his duties as a Customer could be seen as 'extremist' or 'highly unusual' in nature, he could never resign himself to being one of the 'good' guys and go on allowing the UN fully into his life.

To him, the most satisfying thing was the piece of meaning he had been given about the organization when he asked about the name:

"What does *'Buttcheeks'* have to do with it all?" he asked one day while preparing an exotic end cap.

"Absolutely nothing, Clancy," the King he was speaking to answered. "It's *ALL* about the *Customer*..."

These thoughts danced around the fire that was his raison d'etre; winning the Cup for the eighth time, something no one had ever done. Now, winning the Cup in and of itself was not the true reward for Clancy, no. For him, it was a promotion. No, *The* Promotion.

As a King, Clancy joined six others as elite examples of true Customers. Their dress and behavior